CATCH
A CATFISH
KILLER

~~ ~~

ANN M PRATLEY

BY ANN M PRATLEY

Power Moore Investigation Tales
Hoonigan
Resolution of Happiness
Home by the Sea
Tiger in Our House
Catch a Catfish Killer

Forbidden Conflicts Series
Amethyst of Youth
Ruby of Law
Diamond of War
Sapphire of Prejudice
Emerald of Wisdom

Freedom of Flight Series
Christian ~ Brandon ~ Trinity

Painful Deliverance Series
Painful Deliverance
Darkness of Heart
Friendship of Desire

Golden Desires Series
The Golden Desires
The Golden Supremacy
The Golden Unity

Chisholm Manor Series
Alessandra ~ Elizabeth

CHAPTER 1

As Bob Masters entered his apartment, he smiled to himself. Working as an orderly at the local hospital was the job that he'd always wanted, and had always been happy to carry out since he'd secured it five years earlier. It wasn't a job that everyone might have desired, but he enjoyed it enough. There were perks aplenty with the diverse range of people he met and interacted with every day, not to mention the joy he found in the small things that now and then would find their way into his pockets. To all who worked with him, he seemed happy and content. Because of that, everyone appeared to regard him with open friendliness. That - and those little things that might have been in his pocket when he got home at the end of any working day - always kept him happy in his work.

After checking out the day's acquisitions and smiling to himself, Bob tossed his work uniform in the washing machine. Then it was time to indulge in enjoying the heat and pressure of a long, relaxing shower. It was yet another small pleasure, but one he delighted in.

When he'd finally pulled himself from the calming heat of the water, he quickly dressed and made his way into his kitchen.

It was a joy, cooking a decent meal at the end of each working day, but it was also something Bob took pride in. His nature was perfectly suited to the care and attention needed to not only prepare a meal to perfection, but also take the time required to present it equally well. Day to day, night after night, he most often dined alone in the privacy of his small home. That didn't matter. He'd made the choice to live by himself, and although he did get on well with people, he knew he was most suited to bachelor life. Oh, he'd had his fair share of relationships - being 34 years of age, of course he had. Now and then, someone had entered his life who was just that little bit more special than everyone else. On the rare occasion someone had made such an impact on him, he'd enjoyed putting in the time and effort to chase them.

Chase. It was an odd word to use when he took time to consider it. The thrill of the chase. The expression was used a lot, especially in dating. He'd always considered it an odd expression. Maybe that was how it was for cats and mice, and the very reason those cats played with a mouse, taunting it for long periods before seeming to finally decide to kill it. Was it like that within the human race though? Did people truly like to 'chase' others?

Grinning at where his thinking had gone, he refocused on the job at hand. There was a lot that he loved to learn about when it came to the human mind, but no matter what, all humans needed to eat. That consideration was far more important than wondering about one single word of the entire English language.

As his mind centered on the meal he was about to prepare, he felt a calm flow over him. He liked that. Even when he was the only person he was cooking for, it was still worth it for him to present each dish to the highest standard. That was a bi-product of something his mother had taught him: always act as if everyone is watching, even when nobody is. That was her belief - and commitment - right up until the day she'd died at the age of 65.

Although she hadn't lived as long as some, Bob knew his mother had lived a full life. Even on her death bed, she'd reminded him to make the most of however many years he had left in this world. She'd known she was about to leave him and go to be at peace among people she'd loved and lost previously throughout her life. In her final moments, she'd ensured he understood fully what she was saying - that he needed to seize every moment because one day it would all be over with.

When she'd spoken to him that one final time, he'd smiled at her, desperate to make her believe that he was going to be okay. He'd reassured her that after she left him, he would get on with living his life to the fullest, even without her. Only in hindsight could he recognize that he hadn't been honest to her or to himself about that. In truth, since the day she'd died, he hadn't felt entirely like his usual self. Although he demonstrated to others that he was friendly and easy going, and that nothing bothered him, deep inside of him his soul sometimes didn't feel quite as wholesome as others might have thought it would. The small items that made their way to his home after each shift were a small indicator of that truth. Sometimes he didn't even know why he grabbed whatever he did. Did he need such things? No, not usually. Was he hoping to use them in any way in the future? No, not really. The thrill of the chase - perhaps that was the same kind of thinking that he had when he took things from the hospital. Perhaps that very expression wasn't so inaccurate after all.

As he began to prepare the ingredients that he'd purchased on his way home, pushing aside any threat of serious thought further taking over his mind, he felt a familiar excitement flow over him. There was something oddly thrilling about preparing and perfecting a new meal that he hadn't tried before. It wasn't quite as exciting as other parts of his life, but it was a close second. The other aspects of life that were far more enjoyable, he'd learned to compartmentalize in his mind. When he was involved in them, he was all in. Every other hour of the day, however - the hours when he wasn't doing that particular thing - he'd trained himself to forget all about it.

Tasks had to be embarked upon. Jobs needed to be completed. As much as he enjoyed having a range of things that occupied his thoughts at different times, he took pride in his commitment to only focus on what he was doing at the present moment. There was a time for everything. That was another thing his mother had instilled into him - don't fall for all that 'multitasking' hype. Do one thing at a time, and do it with as close to perfection as is humanly possible. In her honor, that was exactly what Bob always tried to do. Sure, sometimes his mind drifted when he wanted to remain focused. Even so, he kept trying to stay on one path at a time. He wasn't perfect, but he could always try his best to at least look like he was set on attempting to be.

Chopping the onions to uniform size, he felt his usual reaction of teary eyes. In response to feeling it happen, he chuckled to himself. He knew that he had a great life, despite how others might view him, living as quietly as he appeared to. Although he'd felt in his youth that he'd never be loved or even wanted by anyone romantically, in recent times his thinking on that had started to turn around. He'd had a few relationships over the years, even though they'd each ultimately failed. Now a new chapter had begun in his life, and it had him feeling not only like he was a new man, but sometimes like he was an entirely new person. It resulted in a strange blend of sadness for the person he'd once been, and happiness for who he'd become - or, at least, the person that people *thought* he'd become.

Once again pushing aside his sliver of realization that much about who he was wasn't quite the truth, he forced the positive side of his mind to remain the predominant one. As he felt tears work harder to push through and come forth, there was absolutely nothing to cry about at that moment in time - only the rigid and strict chopping of onions to one perfect size and shape. Everything else he had going on was in perfect alignment with where he wanted it all to be. He knew what he wanted in his life, and he was on a solid journey to get it. It had taken some learning to figure people out, with their ways of saying one thing and then doing something that went completely against what they'd just said. Now that he had - now that he'd worked out an equation that almost always seemed to result in a very positive outcome for himself - his confidence in that aspect of his life was impressive.

Sensing his thinking threatening his focus yet again, he shook his head, as if to shake away the effect the onions were having on his eyes. No, there was nothing to cry about in his life. Once he'd taken his time to fully enjoy cooking and eating his meal, he'd sit down at his computer and indulge in the evening's pleasure. It was a relatively new hobby of his, but one he couldn't deny suited him well. There were many hours in the day when he was around lots of people. During those times, he loved the presence of others around him. Outside of work, there was calm - and a thrill - in not being in the presence of any other human being.

After moving on to chop, slice and ready all other ingredients needed for his evening meal, he finally grabbed his oversized frypan out of the cupboard and then turned to face his gas range.

Turning the control dial, then pressing the ignition button to activate the flame, that was the last thing that Bob Masters ever saw.

CHAPTER 2

"Good to see you both looking so energized and ready to work," Sarah Johnson said as she addressed the two agents who sat in front of her. Having summoned them to her office, she always found some pleasure in watching how Special Agent Tim Moore and Special Agent Ashley Power interacted with one another.

"As always, Boss," Tim replied, delivering his usual stunning grin.

Ashley smiled at her partner's over-confidence. At the start of each case, she knew he could be cocky, and he could also be a bit of a jokester. They weren't traits she'd ever particularly liked in anyone but, for whatever reason, she didn't mind them in him. Once any investigation got underway, she knew Tim got just as serious about the case as she did. Out of all the partners she'd worked with during her time at the Bureau of Investigation, she had to admit he was the one she felt she worked best with. They both had their little personality quirks that were unique to each of them, but seemed to work well when blended with the quirks of the other. It made researching and working things out even more interesting, with so often being thrown a perspective that was completely different. It also made the thrill of investigations even more enjoyable.

"Focus, Moore," Ashley heard Sarah say in her usual serious tone. "I'm sending you two to investigate a suspicious death."

"Death?" Ashley asked, surprised. "Confirmed?"

"Yep," Sarah said as she produced a buff-colored manila folder and slid it across the desk to the agents. "I know it's been a while since you two had to investigate something like this, but I have no doubt you're the right agents for this job."

"Okay," Ashley said as she reached forward and picked up the folder. She was never entirely sure why she and Tim were 'the right agents' for any particular job and, admittedly, sometimes she found herself wanting to ask her boss how that assessment was even made. As quickly as she found herself wondering about that very question once again, she forced herself to focus on what she'd been presented with.

Flicking through the few pages that were housed within the lightweight cardboard, she couldn't help but ask the obvious question.

"Gas explosion?" she asked and saw Sarah nod. "I'm assuming something about this means it couldn't have just been an accident? Not a simple gas line fault?"

"It certainly could turn out to be, but there are serious questions being asked about that. Fire scene investigators will be doing their part down there, as are the local law enforcement, but your investigative skills will be appreciated, I'm sure," Sarah replied. "Hence why you two need to stop sitting around here, go and get packed, and then get going. It's a four-hour drive south, but you'll get there with plenty of daylight hours left to get straight onto it."

"Four hours?" Tim asked, delivering a cheeky smile to his boss. "We can't fly there instead?"

As he asked the question, he forced himself to try and wipe the smile off his face. Whenever he tried to be cheeky to his supervisor, Sarah always delivered him the coldest stone face that he'd ever seen on anyone. She never seemed able to completely hide her slight amusement, revealing just a hint of happiness in her eyes, but she definitely tried hard to occasionally answer Tim's questions with what some might describe as a glare.

"Nice try, Moore," Sarah finally replied. "That is *not* gonna happen, as I'm sure you already know."

"Okay, well, if we've got a four hour drive ahead of us, we definitely should get going," Ashley said as she stood up, holding the file safely in her hands. Even though there were always digital copies of what they were given to begin with, she'd learned over her years of working on investigations with Tim that he couldn't be trusted with paper. He could literally grab a piece of pristine paper, hand it back seconds later, and it would be a mess. No, she had learned to hold anything papery safely in her own hands if she ever intended to read it herself. "Anything else we need to know?"

"All that I know is what's in there," Sarah replied, nodding toward the folder. "Report to the local precinct when you arrive. Sergeant Pete Thoms is expecting you. I know the file is scant in details right now but hopefully, by the time you get there, they'll have some more information to provide to you."

Ashley watched Tim deliver a silly and completely unnecessary salute to Sarah before he turned and began walking out of the office. The sight made Ashley shake her head and roll her eyes. Yes, her partner could be an idiot. To her relief, he could also be brilliant at reading people, which meant he could also be brilliant at doing his job.

Once both agents were walking down the sterile corridor, Tim turned to face Ashley. He was about to ask her the same question that he always did. He chuckled as he realized that this time he couldn't even manage to get the words out before his partner spoke, directly answering the question that hadn't yet been voiced out loud.

"Don't even think about asking, Special Agent Timothy Moore," Ashley said, smiling wryly at him. "I drive. *Always!*"

Tim laughed out loud. He, too, knew they each had individual personality traits which provided some interesting moments when they worked together. Even though they sometimes amused one another, he couldn't deny that when they got involved in a case, they did work extremely well together.

"See you at yours in half an hour," he heard Ashley call out as she began to walk to one side of the carpark.

"Yep," he called back before embarking on the journey to his own car.

As he walked across the broad Bureau carpark, he felt content in his life, and he felt exhilarated to be heading off on another case. Some people didn't enjoy their work, spending every day going through the same old motions and never truly liking anything at all about how they spent most of their waking hours. That wasn't how Special Agent Tim Moore felt. He absolutely loved his job. It wasn't easy, and there were certainly days when he was sure that no human should ever see the sights that he and Ashley did. Even so, at the end of each case, they knew they'd helped someone in some way. In some cases, it was too late to help the victims, but even in those instances, it made him proud to have provided some kind of justice or peace to victims' loved ones. That kept Tim very happy to keep doing what they did.

CHAPTER 3

"Welcome," Ashley and Tim heard when they entered the destination police station several hours later. "I'm Sergeant Pete Thoms," the gentleman in front of them added as he held out his hand to each of them. "Thanks for coming all this way to assist with this case. I know you've had to travel quite some distance."

"Thank you, Sergeant..." Ashley began to say.

"Just call me Pete," the sergeant said as he led Ashley and Tim into an office and then closed his office door. "Everyone here does, with it being such a small town."

"Thank you, Pete," Ashley said. "I'm Ashley Power, and this is Tim Moore."

As Ashley settled into the chair and watched the sergeant sit down behind his desk, she cast her mind back to all that she and Tim had read about the case they'd been assigned. As seemed usual in the cases that she and Tim were assigned to, there hadn't been too much to go on in the beginning. Part of the thrill that Ashley got from being on cases was trying to figure out a little bit more, and then a bit more still.

"We've read some details about this case, but in the file we've been given, I'm not sure why we've been called in to investigate this," she said. "Can you explain the situation to us in your words?"

The sergeant leaned back in his chair and took his time glancing from one agent to the other before replying.

"There was an explosion in a private residence close to here," he began. "When the fire department finally got in there to put the fire out, one adult male body - that of Mr Bob Masters - was retrieved from what was left of the home."

"And it has been confirmed that the fire resulted from a gas explosion?" Tim asked.

"Yes," the sergeant replied. "Fire investigators were called in to do their assessment. You'll get far more in-depth detail about that when you speak directly to them, but from what I understand, it is their firm opinion that the explosion was intended."

"And it's expected that the explosion was intended for the purpose of murdering Mr Masters, rather than it being either accidental that he was inside when it happened, or he was deceased before the explosion and the fire was used as a way to hide a murder?" Ashley asked.

"Any of those scenarios could be a strong possibility, of course, but at this early stage of this investigation we do believe it was someone's intention to kill Mr Masters with the explosion," the sergeant said. "I recommend you go and talk to the scene investigators. They're at the town fire station at the moment, I believe. If you head over to North Road, you can't miss it. In charge of the region's fire department is Captain John Rogers. He's not a scene investigator, but he's the man to speak to if you want to talk to the fire department head."

After waiting for a long moment in the hope that the sergeant would give them more details, Ashley smiled and stood. It seemed so little that they were beginning their investigation with, and even the police didn't seem to have made any headway in finding much out so far, but Ashley knew she and Tim had started from scratch on cases before. They could certainly do it again.

"Okay, well, thank you, Pete," she said, holding out her hand to him. "We'll go and have a chat to the fire investigators and see where we can go from there."

As Tim stood, he turned to face the sergeant, one question already prominent in his mind.

"It seems as if this might turn out to be a case of murder, but no suspects so far that you're aware of?" he asked, curious about what might have been the aspect of the explosion that had resulted in the Bureau being called upon to investigate.

"As yet, we've only gotten as far as waiting for the scene investigators to do their report," the sergeant replied. "There's no criminal record for Mr Masters and, as far as we know, he's been working as an orderly at the hospital. I went down to his workplace as soon as he was identified, and his supervisors have only spoken well about him. There's nothing that's been mentioned that would indicate foul play from anyone he works with. Not that *that* necessarily means anything, as I'm sure you'll agree."

"And his family?" Ashley asked, nodding. "Partner?"

"None, that we could find," the sergeant replied. "As much as everyone at the hospital seemed to praise Mr Masters for his work ethic and his cheery personality, nobody has ever heard him talk about any living family, or a significant other. The only family records we found in our system were for his parents, who both appear to now be deceased."

"Has an autopsy been done on the victim?" Tim asked.

"Yes," Pete replied. "The final report has yet to come in but the medical examiner has said that first impressions indicate the victim was most likely alive when the explosion happened. It seems he might have been standing right at the point where the blast occurred. We should get confirmation later today of the ME's final assessment. That'll tell us for sure whether the explosion itself was what killed him."

"Definitely no chance of the fire being the cover-up of a murder that had already taken place then," Ashley surmised.

"We don't believe so in this case, no," Pete replied.

"Right. Thank you, Sergeant," Tim said. "We'll be in touch when we have something to share with you."

No more words were spoken as he and Ashley made their way out of the office, and out of the station. Once settled into Ashley's car, Tim turned to face her.

"Tell me again why we're here," he said, not hiding the confused look on his face.

Ashley grinned at him before starting the engine.

"Sometimes, Timmy Boy, that question is the very last one to be answered," she said. She had no idea where their questioning and investigation might lead, but that kind of surprise was always part of the fun.

CHAPTER 4

"Hi, I'm Captain John Rogers," Tim and Ashley heard after they were escorted through the lower level of the North Road Fire Department and into an office upstairs.

"Hello, Captain Rogers, I'm Special Agent Ashley Power, and this is my partner, Special Agent Tim Moore," Ashley said as she shook hands with the man who'd greeted them.

"I'm guessing you're here about the fire that killed Bob Masters," the captain said as he indicated for the agents to sit down on the seats facing his.

"Yes," Tim said. "We understand the scene investigation carried out by the inspectors revealed concerns that the fire may not have been an accident?"

"Yep," the captain replied. "You've just missed the inspectors. They're already on their way back to the city, but I have the full report here. It's quite a bit of a read, I'm afraid, but to sum up, the investigators found evidence that the gas line had been tampered with. Why Bob Masters didn't smell the gas in the house when he entered, we don't know, but as soon as he began to cook his dinner … well…"

Ashley nodded. She had no desire to ponder the depth of destruction the explosion had delivered to the victim. That was something that other members of the Bureau would be assigned to investigate. Ashley just wanted to get on with finding out who might have wanted him dead.

"And there's no possible way that this could have been an accident?" she asked, wanting to ensure she had absolute facts. "No chance that the gas line had corroded due to age, or anything else along those lines?"

"No, Ma'am," the captain replied as he shook his head. "The investigators said that line was cut clean through, most likely with a knife or a box-cutter. You're welcome to take this copy of the report," he said as he nudged the paper stack across the table. "Like I said, it's quite a bit of reading, but you're welcome to take this copy for your investigation."

"Thank you," Tim said as he reached forward and pulled the hefty weight of paper toward him. "Did you know Mr Masters personally?"

"No, I never met him," the captain said. "From what I understand, apart from his work at the hospital, he seemed to keep pretty much to himself. Even though this is a small town, I don't believe our paths ever crossed." He took a long while to study the agents in front of him before he spoke again. "Don't take this the wrong way, but it seems a big deal that the Bureau would be called in to investigate this. Why exactly are you here?"

Ashley nodded at him. Although she silently agreed with what he'd said and what he'd asked, she wasn't sure what to make of the tone that he'd used when he'd spoken.

"With the gas line being cut, and Mr Masters having been killed in the blast, at this stage it is a murder enquiry we're pursuing," she said, knowing she wasn't directly answering the question that had actually been asked. "At least until we learn otherwise."

"Yes, well, everything you'll need to know about the blast and its effect on the scene is in there, but if you need anything more, just holler," the captain said, standing as if to clearly signal that their meeting was already over with. "Our part is pretty much done now, but I'm here during regular work hours - and often outside of regular work hours. If I can help out in any way, I'm happy to answer any questions you have."

"Thanks. Can you tell us if there was anything recovered from the scene that might prove useful to our investigation?" Ashley asked. "Is any part of the scene still intact and able to be walked through?"

"No. As far as explosions go, this was a pretty big one, and very effective. As you'll read in that report, the gas seemed to have built up over an extensive period of time, and with no windows or doors left open to air it out, well, the victim and his home didn't really have a chance, to be honest," the captain replied. "There's only rubble left, but nothing substantial. If you know what you're hoping to find, I can send one of our guys to go and look specifically for it among the remains so we're absolutely certain it's not there, but the scene investigators are excellent at their work. They work pretty quickly once they're on site, but they're also thorough." He paused again before continuing. "What exactly are you thinking might prove useful to your investigation?"

"Computer, or maybe the victim's phone?" asked Ashley, once again disregarding the verbal tone that seemed to convey an underlying expression of her and Tim not being entirely welcome.

"No sign of anything like that was recovered intact, as far as we know," John replied, shaking his head. "The investigators were able to determine what happened to the gas line, but they haven't mentioned having found any intact devices in their report. Nothing like that survived, that our guys were able to see. With the home being so small, so old, and of timber construction, it went up *fast*."

"Thank you," Tim said after a long pause. "We'll have a thorough read through this, and will no doubt be in touch with questions later on," he added before he and Ashley excused themselves and walked out.

"Where to start?" Ashley pondered when they were settled into her car again.

"Seems we've got quite some light reading to do," Tim said as he glanced at the hefty paper file in his hands. "Other than that, the victim's digital footprint is always a useful place to start. No chance of getting our hands on the devices themselves, if any that the victim owned were cremated in the fire, but I'll get the tech guys onto looking into the most recent text messages, phone calls, and social media of the victim."

"Good idea," Ashley agreed. "With Mr Masters having apparently been spoken about so well to everyone who's been asked about him, let's go and visit his workplace first thing in the morning as well. I know Sergeant Thoms said he'd already done so, but it'd be good to learn more about the victim from his peers. Despite what we've heard so far, maybe there's something not so perfect that we'll find he's kept hidden."

"If there's one thing we know all too well from this job, Ash, it's that *nobody* is perfect," Tim said, curious about what kind of journey their investigation was going to take them on.

Ashley nodded but didn't reply. She, too, was unsure of what lay ahead. That was just the kind of case she loved. The more they had to work out, the better.

CHAPTER 5

As Ashley and Tim sat together in Tim's hotel room later that night, both remained silent for a long while, absorbed in their reading. Between the report they'd received from John Rogers, and all of the other documentation they'd been provided with, reading alone seemed an intense job that had to be done.

"There's nothing in his text messages or call log that looks suspicious, exactly. Texts are all pretty standard, and even though we can't know what was talked about in any of these calls, there's no pattern of any particular number appearing too often, or too close in time to the explosion," Ashley said after she'd perused the months worth of information they'd been provided with. "He might have been quite a hit with the ladies though," she added. "His messages to a range of different women make him sound like he was trying to be Mr Darcy!"

"Mr who?" Tim asked, looking up at her with an amused look on his face. As serious as their cases always were, on occasion it was nice to take a breather from the seriousness, even if only for a few seconds at a time.

"Mr Dar..." Ashley began to respond before she realized he was teasing her. "I'm not biting to that one, Moore."

Tim grinned at her before refocusing and thinking about what she'd just told him.

"Yeah, I agree with you," he said. "Looking

through his social media, for months now this guy has been posting content that makes him look like he's the purest gentleman around, and somewhat of a good catch too."

"Liked by all then," Ashley said.

"I'm not so sure about that," Tim replied. "Amongst all of what I've got here, his photos and profile descriptions have been duplicated over several accounts, but with slight variations depicting who exactly he was. He seems to have been trying to pretend to be more than one kind of person - maybe to reach different kinds of audiences?"

"He has more than one social media account to his name, do you mean?" Ashley asked and saw Tim shake his head.

"No, and yes," said Tim. "Similar but not quite the same. Each one seems to have a different *personality*."

"Hmm, but why would an orderly at a hospital need more than one identity?" Ash pondered. "Identification fraud?"

"I don't think so - well, not quite," Tim replied as he studied the open windows on his laptop. "Come have a look at this."

After Ashley moved to where he was, and took some time to look at what he was showing her, she felt her intrigue grow.

"Three versions of Bob Masters," she said, glancing from one account to the next. "He keeps his own name though. Isn't that a bit weird if he wants to present himself as different people?"

"From what I've gathered from these profiles, I do think he was trying to present different *versions* of himself to different audiences," said Tim. "Look. In this one here he looks like a debonair gentleman of maybe 45 or 50 years old. In this one, though, he looks like he's probably aiming to look 35..."

"He was 34," Ashley said, prompting Tim to nod and continue.

"Right, but look at the clothing in this profile - and even the background," Tim continued. "This profile looks like it was designed to attract someone younger. The profile wording for each of these is slightly different, too, like he was going out of his way to appeal to different age groups of followers."

"Hmm," Ashley began as she thought about possibilities. "It's not unheard of, though, for people to steal someone else's photos and name, and then set up a duplicate account online, pretending to be that person. Could it be that at least a few of these profiles were set up by other people? Do we need to find out if Bob Masters was actually behind *any* of them?"

"You're right about people stealing others' photos and using them to create new social media accounts, pretending to be those people, and that *is* a common thing to happen these days - but in this case, I don't think so," Tim replied. "Look at this column here," he added, pointing at the screen. "Every one of these social media accounts was set up and later regularly accessed through the same IP address."

"So probably at the same *actual* address," Ashley surmised.

"Correct," Tim confirmed. "This IP address is the one that the tech guys have identified as the one of Masters' permanent broadband at his home address. All of these profiles do seem to have been created and used by him on his home computer. They haven't all been used at the same time - it looks like one's been set up and used a lot, then another's been set up and used a lot, and then another, and so on. It's possible he's set them up, used them for however long it took to do whatever he wanted to do with that profile, and then moved on, although why he hasn't taken any down, I have no idea. It's as if he just stops checking in to them once he gets caught up in the next profile."

As Ashley scrolled through and studied each profile more thoroughly, she remembered something she'd seen in the hundreds of messages she'd scoured.

"In his text messages, there was a repeating reference to a loan," she said as she looked for one example of what she wanted to find. "Here. *'As soon as you can send me the $1000, I'll be able to get my car fixed and come see you'.*"

"Yeah? Let me see that, Ash," Tim asked. After studying what she'd pointed out, he looked back at his laptop screen. "The date and time for this coincides with this profile here," he said as he pointed. "Over the time that this one was heavily active, he messaged more than twenty different women, all around his age. All of them, he looks like he was trying to get money out of."

"Do we know if he succeeded?" Ashley asked.

"We'll have to wait to get his bank records before we can be a hundred per cent sure of that," Tim replied. "It definitely looks like Bob Masters was a master of luring in at least some young women, though."

"To get money?" Ashley asked as she looked at the range of victim's profile photos. "But he's a good looking guy, and he had a good job that, from what I understand from the file notes, paid him pretty well. Why would he need to get cash from other people?"

"Your guess is as good as mine, Ash, but hopefully tomorrow we'll have the bank records for him," Tim said. "After we have those, we'll have a better idea about one motive that someone might have wanted him dead."

"A woman who's been scorned in some way?" Ashley suggested.

"Maybe," Tim replied. "Or a woman who's been ripped off, having fallen for his charm and paid him money, just like he asked for. If that's the case, maybe he chose the worst target he could have."

"Seems a bit extreme to plan to kill someone, even if it was over money," said Ashley. "I mean, I can imagine someone getting pissed off if one of these women found out that he was chatting to these other women, but killing over a thousand bucks? Sure, it's a lot of money to most people, but murder? It's so little to worry about in the big scheme of things, especially considering a charge for murder could result in life in prison."

"True, but our job has shown us plenty of times that there's no such thing as extreme when it comes to crime, Ash," Tim said. "You know that. All it takes is the right match to strike the right flint."

Ashley looked at him and rolled her eyes in mock horror.

"Nice play on words, Partner, but completely inappropriate, given how our victim died," she said, pretending to chastise him. "Okay, well, at least we have a possible reason about why our victim might have been killed. It's a start. We need to look into these women that he's had contact with. If there's any possibility that this guy did choose the wrong woman to lead on and then use for his own financial gain, we need to find her. Otherwise, who knows who else might suffer if she again gets pissed off by some guy chatting to her on the Internet."

"Yep. We need to focus on all the women that Bob Masters asked for money," Tim agreed. "It's not much to go on, and it might not have anything to do with this case at all, but it'll be worth it to look into, even if it just means ruling out any of these women as suspects."

CHAPTER 6

Over breakfast the following morning, Ashley and Tim scoured the bank statements they'd received via email overnight. Although they knew there was always a chance that someone with financial criminal intent could have hidden bank accounts somewhere, they equally knew it was worth looking through the accounts that were easily visible.

"Our victim wasn't much of a shopper," Ashley said before she took a sip of her second cup of coffee. "Even though we can see he was getting paid pretty well by the hospital, and he's got these other deposits of cash going in, there's hardly any spending recorded, other than the general basics - phone, gas and power bills; house payments; charges at the supermarket. Does anyone really live like that?"

Tim studied her face as he pondered the question.

"I'm sure some people do," he said. "But I don't think Bob Masters was one of those people."

"What are you thinking?" Ashley asked, always eager to hear her partner's thoughts.

"Well, we know from his social media, and the online dating accounts of his that we've now found…"

"The ones that we know of," Ashley added.

"Yes, from the ones that we know of - Masters had settled into a pretty well-established routine of using his Internet presences to ask women for money," Tim said and saw Ashley nod. "From these bank accounts - as far as we can tell - he did successfully manage to get the thousand he asked for, from thirteen women that I can see."

"Right," Ashley agreed. "We also know that he asked at least twenty women for that exact sum of money and, of those, thirteen went ahead and paid it to him. Even if that might not be considered a high success rate, that's still thirteen thousand dollars. It's pretty good money for doing nothing more than being nice to lonely women from behind a screen."

"True," Tim said. "We can see that money going into his account, but none of his accounts show much money going out, so I do think it could be likely there've been more victims out there," he suggested. "I think it's quite possible that any cash that he used from day to day, he was getting off other women."

"Or from these ones that we know about?" Ashley wondered.

"Maybe," said Tim. "From all of these messages combined, we can see the spiraling of his charm over some of these earlier women. It looks like he chatted them up, showering them with compliments, until he told them he wanted to see them but couldn't because of car problems. Some were wise enough to question his intentions, so didn't pay him, but others *did* pay him, thinking they'd finally get to meet him after they helped him out. After they sent that money through to him, thinking they were helping him to be able to visit them, his excuses have continued and some of the messages from these women after that indicate they've turned pretty irate."

"As could be expected," Ashley said, feeling an inward anger toward the very person they were trying to find out what had happened to. "But if he was using his car troubles as an excuse not to meet up with them, they must all be from out of town. If they were more local, that excuse wouldn't have worked to begin with."

"True," Tim said, pulling a sheet of paper out of his pocket. "We have the names of the thirteen women here, and Tech are going to be sending through whatever details they can find about where these women are living. We'll hopefully receive those details soon."

"Maybe the thirteenth woman to pay was the one woman he never should have approached," Ashley suggested.

"Agreed," Tim replied. "Maybe, for Mr Bob Masters, thirteen really was a bad luck number."

"Could be, but let's see what the records reveal. Perhaps they'll help us along. I know that if I was in the same position as those women - if some guy who I'd connected with online was asking me for money, and then proved to me that he wasn't to be trusted, and instead just wanted to rip me off, I'd be more than a little bit pissed off," Ashley said as she felt a shudder pass through her. She hadn't even considered the idea of trying to meet people through the Internet. It was something that, when she momentarily pondered the possibility, she really couldn't find any enthusiasm for. "In the meantime, while we wait for those details to arrive," she continued as she dismissed even the thought of such an idea. "Eat up. We've got an investigation to get on with."

Tim smiled at her. She was an interesting person to work with. Sometimes she sounded like she had ants in her pants, and was itching to get on with the next stage in an investigation. At other times, he knew she could get despondent, especially when cases were slow to gain momentum. At those times, he wished she wasn't so hard on herself, but he'd long ago accepted that she was. That was just part of who Special Agent Ashley Power was.

CHAPTER 7

"We've got the addresses of eighteen easily-accessible targets of Bob Masters that we have evidence of him *trying* to get money out of," Tim said as he and Ashley climbed into the car to begin visiting people on their list. "Eighteen people that he tried to get the same, clean, one grand out of."

"But he only succeeded in getting cash out of thirteen, right?" Ashley asked, curious about the numbers Tim was talking about.

"We've seen that he was definitely successful in getting money out of those thirteen, but of those, we've only got contact details for four so far. The fifth that we'll visit today was asked for money but I can't see any evidence that she did pay him," Tim replied. "The rest, I've gotten the tech guys to reach out to via their social media accounts. Hopefully those people will get back to us soon. In the meantime, these five are within a two-hour drive radius, so I think it'll be worth going to visit them. That should give us enough time to also go to the hospital and see if we can find anyone who thought Bob Masters *wasn't* a perfect guy."

"Okay, yeah, that sounds like a good plan. If he had an unhealthy association in his thinking about women, there might be someone in his workplace who's picked up on that," Ashley said as she started the engine. "One thing at a time though!" she added, securing her seatbelt. "I have to admit, it feels weird to even think about going to visit people that were sucked in through social media."

Tim turned and grinned at her. In many ways, she looked like a sophisticated woman who'd be up to date with everything technological. He loved that very little about technology had changed who Ashley was in her heart. Through all of their interactions with technology and 'the digital age', she'd been very glad to leave any investigation up to the tech professionals, quietly displaying that she actually knew very little about it at all.

CHAPTER 8

"Victim number one of Bob Masters - Jane Mundo, twenty-nine," Tim said as they pulled up to a large home on the outskirts of the next town over. "Wow. I'm guessing this woman really does have some serious money," he added as he looked up at the large structure in front of them. He wasn't surprised at the word 'palatial' appearing in his thoughts as he viewed the home.

Ashley nodded but didn't reply with words. Looking at the prominent three-storied home, with its solid stone walls and no sign of any neighbors immediately nearby, she was surprised.

"Makes me wonder why someone living like this would even *want* to meet someone online," Tim muttered. When he saw Ashley turn and look at him, he continued. "Surely anyone who lives like this could have anyone they wanted."

"You might think that," Ashley said. "Then again, if you had this kind of wealth, who would - *could* - you truly trust? Wouldn't you *always* expect someone to be trying to steal your money? Maybe getting to know someone online provides the exact smokescreen that someone with this kind of wealth could use to their advantage. It's easy to hide who you really are if you're sitting behind a screen. While I'm sure there are plenty of people pretending online to be wealthier than they really are, I'm guessing there are just as many wealthy people who like the idea of pretending to be *poorer* than they really are. I think if it was me, I'd expect anyone to want to try and steal from me if they knew I was this kind of rich."

"Yeah, you and I might expect it, but maybe this person didn't think that," Tim said. "If they did, surely they shouldn't have been able to so easily be ripped off."

"Maybe a grand is nothing to someone like this," Ashley pondered out loud. "Maybe she wasn't ripped off, and instead just felt okay with giving a complete stranger that thousand."

"True, but let's stop playing the 'maybe' game, Partner," Tim said before unlatching his door. "Only one way to find out exactly what kind of person Ms Mundo is. Let's go!"

After being escorted into the large open foyer of the beautiful home, Tim and Ashley were invited to sit in a small lounge and present their questions.

"I heard about Bob on the news," the young woman said as she faced the agents. "I assume that's why you're here? You know that I'd been chatting to him online?"

Surprised by the woman's directness, Tim blinked and studied her face before he replied. It was never a given how someone being questioned was going to respond. He was sometimes saddened when he realized he'd grown to expect people to want to hide things they'd done, rather than admit things.

"Your name did show up as someone he'd interacted with, yes," he said. "Can you tell us about your relationship with him?"

"Relationship?" the young woman asked as she scoffed. "I'm not sure that's the word I'd use! But what can I say? I connected with Bob through an online dating site - Date Today. He seemed nice enough, so I didn't see anything wrong with it, or with him. He stood out as someone who was eloquent in the way he spoke, and he did seem to have some interest in the issues of the world, so I guessed he must have been a guy who watched the news every night. Intelligent too, I thought. He was … well, let's just say he was a cut above most of the guys I'd interacted with in that site."

As she spoke, Tim continued to study her face, curious about why someone so young, so attractive, and obviously so well off, would need to go near a dating website at all.

"And things went well?" Ashley asked and saw the young woman nod.

"Yes, like I said, he was good to talk to," Jane replied. "He seemed … mature, I guess is the way I'd describe him. There was never any of the usual immaturity that guys often show in there. Not once did he mention body parts, or ask for a hookup. He genuinely seemed like he was just a nice guy. Thoughtful, intelligent, charming, and respectful. There was never anything to make me think he was anything other than all of those - not at the start anyway."

"Did you and Mr Masters meet up in person?" Tim asked.

"No," Jane replied. "I kept thinking we were going to meet, but then he had a lot of reasons *not* to meet. At first, I believed them. I mean, life is so frigging stressful and busy for all of us, right?! After a while, it did seem more and more like he just wasn't interested in meeting me in person at all. They seemed endless - his excuses for not getting together. To be honest, I gave up on him being someone I'd ever meet, long before our final interaction."

"Right. Can you tell us what kind of excuses he would make with regards to meeting you?" Ashley asked and saw the young woman shrug her shoulders.

"You name it. He seemed to have every reason under the sun for not trying to make it happen," Jane replied. "Initially, like I said, I didn't mind that too much. At first, I genuinely thought we'd get around to making it happen sooner or later. It was quite a while - I don't remember exactly how long now - but yeah, quite a while before I gave up on him."

"And you made a payment to him?" Tim asked. In response to his question, he saw Jane take some time to contemplate her answer before she replied.

"I did," she finally said as she glanced down at her hands on her lap. "Friends said I was silly to do that, but over time he did convince me that he needed it to come and see me. Even though my gut told me that he wasn't ever going to actually meet me, when he asked … I don't know. He'd been so nice and charming, and I just thought, 'why not'. I'm sure it sounds silly. Even as I say that, it sounds silly to *me*! I suspected he wasn't being truthful about needing the money to see me, and he never intended to see me, but when he asked, I still didn't say no."

"You really don't think that he intended to meet you, Jane? Ever?" Ashley asked, curious.

"No," Jane admitted.

"Did he ask you for more money after getting that initial payment from you?" asked Tim.

"No," Jane replied. "To be honest, that did surprise me, but it was only the one thousand that he seemed to be interested in. Seems crazy, since I'd already proven I was willing to hand money over to him, but maybe that's part of his act - always be sure to only ask for one payment. Anyway, after I sent the money through to him, his manner and tone changed. It didn't entirely surprise me because I'd already given up hope by then, but it did sadden me."

"How so?" Tim asked.

"Oh, I mean he was still friendly enough, but … I dunno … there was just something different about how he chatted to me. And even though he had the cash to get his car fixed, he then just had more excuses to not meet up. I'd already had my suspicions before I paid him, but that was the point when I finally admitted to myself that there was no doubt he had just used me for the money. That was the point when I had to admit to myself just how completely *stupid* I was," she said as she rolled her eyes. "But, we do stupid things sometimes, right? All we can do is pick ourselves up and move on."

"And have you?" asked Ashley. "Moved on?"

"Oh, yes," Jane replied. "I learned a lesson from that instance. I pulled my dating profile down and haven't looked back. I won't make that mistake again, even if I do ever return to the site."

"Can I ask … and forgive me for being so forward. I don't mean to cause offence…" Tim began to say before he saw her smile at him, as if she was reading his mind and knew exactly what question was coming.

"Why did I go into that dating site?" Jane asked. "Don't worry. Plenty of people who know about my time in there have asked me that. To answer your unspoken question, I was lonely."

"You're not … married?" asked Ashley, already knowing the answer.

"Yes, I'm married. I'm married to a good man who is a lot older than me," Jane replied. "And yes, he knew what I was doing. At his request, I didn't give him specific details about who I was chatting to, but when we married, he made it clear that he was past being able to … do things in the bedroom. He wanted a wife, but I think he likes me being on his arm most of all. Don't get me wrong - he's a wonderful man and he's only ever been good to me, but it was accepted as part of our marriage that if I needed … the physical stuff … I could go out and find it, so long as I was discrete and nobody else would ever know."

"How do you think that made your husband feel when you actually went on the dating site and did it?" Tim asked. "Someone thinking they'll be able to accept a situation, isn't always how they feel when it actually happens and becomes a reality."

"Yeah, I know," Jane said. "But, honestly, he's been fine. I mean, I didn't go out and show myself off with a different guy on my arm. I was only chatting online, and my profile was only shown to people I wanted to see it, so friends and colleagues of my husband's never would have seen it…"

"That you know of," said Tim. "I'm guessing you'd never know for sure who was behind a profile you were interacting with."

"Yes, that's true, and that was a slight concern for me," Jane said. "It was all very discrete, but as it turned out, Bob was the first and only guy I was interested in meeting in person, and I didn't end up meeting him anyway."

"Does your husband know that you paid some money to Mr Masters?" Ashley asked.

"No," Jane replied. "Not that I know of, anyway. We don't have a joint bank account. When I married, my husband set up an account for me, which is paid into each week from a trust of his. It's kind of like … I guess you'd call it an *allowance* that I get. I don't think he has access to the account itself … but I suppose I can't be a hundred percent sure of that."

"How do you think he *would* react if he knew that you'd paid money to another man?" Tim asked.

Jane studied the agents facing her. When she'd seen the news about the death of the guy she'd been chatting to, she'd wondered if she should approach law enforcement and admit that she'd spoken to him online. She wasn't at all surprised by the agents turning up at her home. She *was* surprised by the direction their questions had turned.

"Please tell me you don't think my *husband* could have something to do with Bob's death," she said after a long period of silence.

"We don't think that, but of course we have to consider and investigate all possibilities," Ashley said.

"No," Jane said. "No! He is a good man. He wouldn't do anything to hurt anyone!"

Seeing the young woman beginning to get angry at such a thought, Tim took some time to further study her. While the purpose of questioning was to get answers, he liked that sometimes the answers came not from the words spoken, but the way that the person being interviewed looked and sounded in their responses.

"Your husband is wealthy," Tim said quietly. "There's no chance that he could pay someone…"

"No!" the young woman exclaimed as she stood up. "I'm sorry, but no. When I said that my husband would never hurt anyone, that includes the possibility of him paying someone *else* to hurt someone. No, there is nothing to even look at here."

"Alright, well, we won't take up any more of your time. Thank you for speaking to us, Mrs Mundo," Ashley said after glancing at Tim and seeing he had no more questions for the woman who was clearly upset. "We'll leave you now."

No more words were said as the agents were shown to the door. Once outside, Tim turned to face Ashley.

"Thoughts?" he asked her, still uncertain about the authenticity of the woman they'd just met.

"As much as she made it sound like her husband wouldn't have cared about her interacting with men online, I don't think there's any harm in delving into the background of her and Mr Mundo, just in case," Ashley said as they climbed into the car. "I'm not sure that will lead us anywhere new, but nothing to lose in checking it out, right?"

"True," Tim agreed. "I'll get head office to look into his background, and his financial records if they can. While they do that, we have another four women to visit and have a chat with about Bob Masters."

"Yes, let's see if we can find one who actually met this guy," Ashley said. "I mean, was he literally just chatting to these women so that he could get money from them, and managed to do that without actually meeting *any* of them?"

"Only one way to find out," Tim replied as he smiled at her.

CHAPTER 9

"Next one is Neve Cooper," Tim said as they left the fourth woman they'd liaised with about their murder victim. "Last one for the day."

Ashley quietly nodded in reply. It felt like they'd been hearing the same conversation, over and over, with every woman they'd spoken to. For each, Bob Masters had said the same things, following through with the same charm and the same routine until he'd gotten to his point of asking for money. Some women had happily paid out of eagerness and excitement to finally meet him. Others had been uncertain, but had paid anyway. No matter how the flow of actions had gone, it had been interesting for Ashley to hear the women speak about their experiences with the man they'd all connected with through the dating site.

When the agents pulled up at the last address they planned to visit that day, Ashley turned to face Tim.

"Hopefully, this one will provide us with something new," she said before seeing Tim smile at her.

"To be honest, it wouldn't surprise me if they all end up saying the same thing, Ash," he said. "This guy definitely seemed to have a well-planned, well thought-out routine that he adhered to, no matter who he connected with. He knew just what to say, when to say it, and *how* to say it to keep these women on a hook until he felt they were pliable enough and he could get them to give in to what he really wanted -

their money."

"How do you think someone like that keeps on top of all these conversations?" Ashley pondered. "I mean, I know he had different profiles, but with each of those profiles he also had to display a different personality, and he had different targets. Keeping track of what he'd said to each one must have been a *nightmare*. I don't know how he did it."

"Well he clearly didn't always," Tim replied. "If he was exceptional at what he was trying to do, he would have had an even higher success rate in getting money out of these women."

"True," Ashley agreed. "Still, he was doing this around working long hours in a full time job. After running around as a hospital orderly for eight hours, I don't think I'd have the energy to be bothered with this kind of carry on. Those guys work hard! How could anyone be bothered to even try to do this kind of thing while holding down an active full time job? And what was the point anyway, when he was getting paid so well by the hospital, and doesn't seem to have had any financial over-commitment or difficulties?"

"I don't know. I guess some people are just greedy enough to think the time investment is a small price to pay to get what they want, but I understand what you're saying!" Tim said before seeing her smile and open her door to get out.

After walking up the path and then knocking on the front door of the home they stood before, the agents waited a long while before it opened.

"Ms Neve Cooper?" Ashley asked and saw the young woman nod. "I'm Special Agent Ashley Power and this is Special Agent Tim Moore. We'd like to talk to you about a man we believe you were chatting with…"

The young woman looked surprised before she

began to blush.

"If you're referring to my online chatting, I've spoken to *lots* of men over the last couple of years, Agents, so you'll have to be far more specific," Neve replied as she opened her door wider. "But please do come in and tell me what this is all about."

Once all were seated, Ashley began the conversation.

"Do you recognize this man, Ms Cooper?" she asked as she handed Neve a photo.

"Yeah, I think so. That's … Bob?" Neve said and saw both agents nod in confirmation. "He looks quite a bit older there than he did in the photos I've seen, but it does kind of look like him."

"What can you tell us about your interactions with him?" asked Tim.

"Not much to tell, really," Neve replied. "I started chatting to him through one of the dating sites I'm on - I can't remember which one now, sorry. I've been on them all! But yeah, he and I chatted for a bit, but I never actually met him."

"Do you remember why that was?" Tim asked.

"Yeah, I think he was one of those guys who always said he wanted to meet, but never followed through," Neve said. "I've chatted to loads of them who do that, so it wasn't really a big deal, but I lost interest when it was obvious he was after something."

"What do you think it was that he was after?" asked Ashley.

"Money!" Neve replied. "I've been in and out of dating sites for a few years now, and I'm well used to guys showing themselves as users, but usually it's for sex. This guy stood out when he asked me for money. I was so surprised and horrified about it that I told a couple of friends about his reason for needing the money, and got their honest feedback. My friends agreed with my suspicion that I was probably being scammed purely for that reason - money, I mean."

"Were you angry about him asking you for the money?" Tim asked.

"No, not angry," Neve said as she scoffed. "Like I said, I'm well used to chatting to guys who turn out to be users in one way or another. I'm just glad that I had the sense to talk to friends about it and get another perspective. Even though I've connected with loads of guys over the years - probably hundreds, in all honesty - this was actually my first time of being asked for cash. It surprised me a lot when it happened. I wasn't sure, at first, if he was being sincere or not. I don't know why I didn't just assume he was a scammer. Everything makes sense in hindsight! But then again, I guess that's what makes these guys good at what they do - they do a great job of convincing their targets that they're interested in them."

"That is true. What did your friends advise you to do when you told them about your interactions with Mr Masters?" asked Ashley.

"Run!" Neve replied as she chuckled. "No, seriously, they confirmed what I'd been starting to think - that if a guy was asking for money, there was reason to be suspicious, and he wasn't actually interested in me."

"When did you last speak to Mr Masters?" Tim asked.

"Well, we never 'spoke', but chat? Umm, maybe six weeks ago?" Neve said. "I'm not sure exactly, and I do remember deleting him from my dating site conversation log, so I can't check and give you a definite date, sorry, but I'm pretty sure it would be six weeks - maybe five, but definitely not any more recently than that."

"So you never paid him anything?" Ashley asked

and saw the young woman shake her head.

"No, he never got anything out of me," Neve replied. "Did he succeed in getting money from other people? Is that why you're here? Has he pissed someone off and they've reported him?"

At that moment, Tim studied her face, wondering if it could be possible that she hadn't heard about the death of Bob Masters.

"Mr Masters is dead," Ashley replied, also surprised by the young woman's indication that she hadn't yet heard the news.

Both agents watched as the woman's face changed.

"He's …?" Neve began to ask.

"Yes," said Ashley. "You didn't hear about his passing on the news?"

"No, I … I never watch the news. Too depressing," Neve said. "And even though I'd talked about my situation with him to friends, I don't think I shared his name. I hadn't actually met the guy, so if anyone I know saw or heard about his death on the news, they wouldn't have made the connection so wouldn't have known to tell me." She paused a long while before speaking again. "How did he die?"

"He died in a fire," Tim replied, continuing to study the young face before him.

"Oh … shit, that … that's *horrible*," Neve said. "I mean, he obviously wasn't a good person, using women like I think he must have been, but for him to die … wait, are you thinking someone he chatted to through that dating site did that to him?"

"We have to investigate all possible leads, but yes, that is a possibility that we haven't ruled out yet," Ashley replied. "Do you know anyone else from the dating site, who had contact with Mr Masters?"

"No," Neve replied. "I never interacted with the other *women* in there, if that's what you mean. I talk to lots of guys, though. I guess that some of them might know each other, and know *him*, but I don't know about that. At the end of the day, who of us really knows who we've *ever* spoken to online? It's just one aspect of online dating that I've come to realize and accept - never believe anybody is who they say they are until they're right in front of your face. And even then, *still* be wary about whether they're who they say they are. There are so many people out there with bad intentions. I've been lucky, I know. Lots of the guys I've chatted to have obviously been users, and some of them not very nice people, but I know I'm fortunate to have never had anything bad happen to me through this online dating thing." She paused for a long while before speaking again. "He's dead? Shit. I kind of wish I felt glad, like that was karma or something, but I don't. Nobody deserves to die … like … shit, that's horrible."

Ashley and Tim both watched the young woman as she exhibited an array of emotions across her facial expressions. When it seemed like she wasn't going to offer any further information, Ashley spoke.

"Alright, well, we'll leave you now, Ms Cooper," she said as she stood up, not sure there was any further information that the young woman *could* provide at that time. "Thank you."

Neve remained silent and thoughtful as she walked the agents to her front door.

"If I can be of any other assistance, please let me know, but really, I don't think there'd be anything that I know about him that any other woman from the dating site wouldn't know," she said as she watched Ashley and Tim walk out. "To be honest, I didn't even think that would have been his real *name*. So many of them aren't who they say they are. I guess you're wondering why I - why anyone - would even go on dating sites, especially when I know that most of the guys don't even seem real."

"It's not our place to judge," said Tim, delivering an outstanding smile to the young woman. "But be careful."

"Oh, don't you worry - I'm always that!" Neve replied, smiling as if to make a joke out of a subject that she knew might not be considered amusing by anyone else.

"Yes, of course," said Ashley. "Thank you for your time, Neve."

As they headed toward the car, both agents were quiet as they replayed the conversation in their heads once more.

"Well, that's..." Tim finally began to say before he heard his phone sound in his pocket. After taking the call, he climbed into the car and turned to face Ashley. "We've got another one."

"Another victim of Bob Masters to visit?" Ashley asked, impatient to get whatever new details they were being provided with.

"Another burned *body*," Tim said as he secured his seatbelt. "Pete Thoms has suggested we go straight to the scene."

Ashley watched as he typed a new address into the GPS unit on the dashboard.

"He thinks it's the same kind of death?" she asked as they began their journey.

"Yep, another gas explosion in a private home," Tim replied. "Is it possible we've been on the wrong track, talking to all these online scam victims of Bob Masters?"

"Anything's possible. That's always the case, no matter what," Ashley said. "Let's wait and see what this new victim will reveal to us."

"Visiting Bob's work colleagues at the hospital

might have to wait till tomorrow," said Tim.

"Well, that's one place that we *know* will be open all day and all night!" Ashley replied. "We'll get there. For now, let's push Mr Masters to the side of our thoughts."

"Agreed," Tim said, wondering what the likelihood would be that the second victim would have any association to the first.

CHAPTER 10

Even before reaching the address they'd been provided with, Ashley and Tim could smell the distinctive scent of smoke and wet-down smoldering. By the time they got to the residential address, fire crews appeared to already be preparing to leave.

"Thanks for coming," they heard Sergeant Thoms call out as he walked toward them. "It was a hot blaze that caught quick, but the fire fighters were onto it very quickly. Fire investigators are in there now, so it could be a long while before we get their formal report, but first impression, from the head of the crew, indicates that this might be a similar fire to the one that Bob Masters was caught up in."

"And there's a body?" Ashley asked and saw the sergeant nod. "Just one?"

"So far, yes," Pete Thoms replied. "But like I say, the scene's still being investigated, so it will most likely take quite a while yet."

Tim glanced from the sergeant's face to that of Ashley, silently wondering why they'd been summoned to the scene so quickly. It seemed there would be nothing for them to know for quite some time, other than any details they could find out regarding the home owner.

"Lance Summers," the sergeant said, as if reading Tim's thoughts. "That's who owns the place and lives there, according to one of the neighbors who came out and spoke to me," he added before seeing one of the scene investigators approaching.

"I can confirm there's only one body," the investigator said to the sergeant.

"Definite?" Pete asked, just to be sure.

"Yep," replied the investigator. "This scene isn't as bad as the last one, so it's been easier for us to look around in there, but I'm a hundred percent certain there's nobody else in what's left of the house."

"Any chance of an intact phone or computer in there?" Tim asked and saw the investigator look at him with immediate surprise and mild suspicion.

"Special Agents Moore and Power are from the Bureau of Investigation," Pete said. "They're assisting in our investigation about what happened to Bob Masters."

The investigator nodded to each agent before answering Tim's question.

"There is a desktop computer in there," he said. "It hasn't fared well, but isn't completely destroyed so might be able to be salvaged. The victim's phone is in what's left of his pocket. It's just a mangled mess. If you want us to let you know when we're done, we can, if you want to take what's left of the computer."

Tim glanced at Ashley and saw her nod.

"Thank you," Ashley replied. "We can, at least, send it off to our tech guys. Maybe they can't do anything with it, but we'll let them decide."

"No problem," the investigator said, giving Ashley a glance that told her he might not have been assessing her just as an agent at that moment. "When we've finished, I can let you know."

Not particularly liking how the guy in front of him was looking at Ashley, Tim spoke. It wasn't unusual for Ashley to get the attention of people who appeared to be attracted to her. At those times, Tim found himself feeling surprisingly protective over his work partner.

"That would be very helpful, thank you," he said, demanding the investigator's attention shift. "Maybe once you guys are finished, you could take the computer down to the fire department? We can then package it up and dispatch it from there."

The investigator smiled, as if suspecting Tim had taken a dislike to him, before nodding and then moving away.

"Can't you guys check the victim's computer usage remotely anyway?" Pete Thoms asked.

"Our tech guys can look into the victim's online activity, and they will," Tim replied. "It can, however, be good to see what else a computer has been used for, that wasn't done online, but I'm sure anything Mr Summers has done, we will possibly be able to see through his use of the Internet."

"Right," Pete said. "Well, as there doesn't appear to be anything more I can do here, at least for the moment, I'll head back to my office. If I can be of any help to you, I'm guessing you'll let me know." Before he'd taken a few steps, he turned back to them. "Oh, just in case you need it," he said as he reached into his pocket. "This is a copy of a photo of Mr Summers. One of the boys at the station played football with him, it seems, so gave this to me when he heard the news. He said it's a couple of years old but he thought it still might prove useful for the investigation."

"Thank you," Ashley said as she received and studied the photo. "I'm sure this will help us a lot."

Tim and Ashley watched as the sergeant nodded, then left them to go and jump into his car, and leave the scene.

"Looks like the fire investigators are going to be here for quite a while longer," Tim said. "Let's go and chat to some of these neighbors. We know that, at this stage, the investigators think the method of death was similar to Bob Masters. Let's see if there're any other similarities between these two victims."

CHAPTER 11

Knocking on each door of the immediate neighborhood around the crime scene, Ashley and Tim were greeted with a blend of eagerness to help, and evident dislike for any person involved in law enforcement. One by one, each conversation they embarked upon provided no clue about anything that anyone had seen or heard in the hours or days leading up to the explosion. No strange people had been seen walking around the neighborhood. No out-of-place vehicles had been noticed lurking in the immediate area. Overall, talking to the residents of the street where an explosion had just occurred seemed unusually peaceful.

"Speaking to these people isn't looking too helpful, Ash," Tim said as they began walking away from the eighth home they'd visited. "I can't believe nobody saw or heard anything out of the ordinary. Whatever happened to neighbors looking out for each other?"

As Ashley climbed into the driver seat of her car, she considered his question as she thought about the several conversations they'd just had with the people in the area who'd been home. Settled into her seat, she turned to face Tim.

"People work, and people have other things going on in their lives. I'm sure people even noticing their neighbors coming and going these days isn't as easy or common as it once might have been. But worry not, Timmy Boy! We've only just begun," she said, plastering a smile onto her face. "It's way too early to be sounding so defeated!"

"True," Tim replied. He hadn't meant to sound defeated, but he returned her smile before refocusing. "Okay, so, that's all of the houses in the immediate area covered. I've just received notification that some digital info has come through email about this victim. Do you want to go back to the hotel and look through it while we wait for the fire inspectors to finish their examination and get their report through? Or head to the hospital now?"

"Yeah, let's head to the hospital first," Ashley replied. "I think it'd still be good to talk to people who actually knew Bob Masters, and I'm curious to see if any of the women he worked with have anything negative to say about his manner toward them."

"Agreed," said Tim, happy to sit back and realign his thinking with the previous victim rather than the newest one.

CHAPTER 12

"Agents, what can I help you with today?" Ashley and Tim heard a mature woman ask after they'd explained to several staff members the line of enquiry they were hoping to complete at the hospital.

"We were hoping to speak to some of your staff about a Mr Bob Masters," Tim began to say.

"Oh, yes!" the woman said. "Such a terrible thing to happen to someone like that!"

"Someone like that?" asked Ashley.

"Oh, Bob was..." the woman continued as her mouth smiled but her eyes began to moisten. "Let's just say that Bob was a kind soul. Would do anything for anyone!"

"Do you think everyone who worked with him felt that way?" Tim asked and saw the woman nod.

"Oh, yes," she said. "I mean, I can't speak for everyone, of course, but I can confirm that I've been working here on this floor for as long as he was, and I never heard anything bad said about him. Staff and patients alike would all say he was helpful and caring. Such a tragic loss," she added as she shook her head in evident disbelief. "But what exactly would you like to know?"

"We are here only to try and learn more about him," said Ashley. "By all accounts, he does seem to have been regarded very highly by all."

"Yes, like I say, I've never heard a bad word said about him - not from patients or staff," the woman said. "Although…"

"Although what?" Tim asked, his curiosity piqued by the uncertain tone he'd heard.

"Well, a while back … I'm hesitant to say anything about … oh dear … I must say something," the woman said, her voice revealing the hesitancy she appeared to be experiencing. "I don't like to say anything negative about the dead but … some time ago … there was an allegation…"

"Yes?" asked Ashley. "What was the allegation, and who was it made by?"

"Nobody made any formal complaint, as far as I'm aware, but I do remember there was some … speculation … that he might have been stealing things from here," said the woman. "I never believed it myself, of course. Bob steal things? From the *hospital*? No, he was too nice to do that!"

"But nobody reported their suspicions?" asked Tim.

"No, like I say, I never heard of any formal report being made," said the woman. "It was more of a whispering among staff - you know, the *'I think he did that'* sort of thing. As far as I know, it never actually went anywhere."

"Do you know who started saying such a thing about Mr Masters?"

"Hmm, no, not really," said the woman. "By the time it reached me, it had already made the rounds, so it was probably as valuable as those Chinese Whispers kind of things. It could've been blown up to a whole other degree from what had actually happened, so I chose not to believe it. Not Bob. He wasn't a thief. No, I still don't believe it."

"Would you be able to put us in touch with any of the staff members who were talking about it when it happened?" asked Ashley.

"No," the woman replied before stepping up to them and leaning in close. "To be honest, I don't feel right even mentioning it. It was only gossip, and I wouldn't want to ruin someone's good reputation by helping gossip like that continue."

"Of course," said Tim. "We do appreciate that, however it is our job to do a thorough investigation into Mr Masters' death. No matter who did this to him, I'm sure you'd agree it best that we catch this person."

"Oh, yes!" the woman exclaimed. "Yes, of course you must catch and stop him! That's the very least that should be done for such a kind soul as Bob was!"

Ashley and Tim glanced at one another as they waited for the woman to provide names. None were provided before people running past and shouting caught the attention of all.

"I'm sorry," the woman said as she started to move with the other staff members. "I have to go! Please find whoever did this!" she added before disappearing through the large swinging doors at the end of the corridor.

"And I guess that is that," Tim said after the flurry of staff had moved beyond where they stood.

"Yes, I doubt she'll be able to talk to us again - not today anyway," Ashley agreed. "Let's see if we can find anyone else who'd like to talk to us about our Mr Bob Masters."

An hour later, she and Tim were walking out of the large building.

"Three people mentioned the suspicion of Bob Masters stealing things from the hospital, but none of them seemed to have any way of confirming if that actually was happening, or it was just some made-up gossip that someone started," Ashley said as they walked across the vast carpark.

"Yes, whoever started that rumor either doesn't

want to say so, or isn't here today," Tim agreed. "And nobody seemed to know why the suspicions were never officially reported."

"Yes, in a hospital, I would have assumed even the slightest hint of someone stealing anything would have been reported, even if only to have an investigation done that would rule out any possibility of the rumor being true."

"Maybe there was more to Mr Masters than we've yet learned," Tim said. When he saw Ashley halt in her steps and turn to face him, he continued. "What if he was someone who wasn't so nice on the inside? What if he was someone who knew how to manage and control anything like that being said about him, by counter attacking whoever started that rumor?"

"Blackmail, do you mean?" asked Ashley.

"Maybe," said Tim. "It's a long shot, I know, but we already know from his messaging history with women online that Masters definitely had it in him to try and get what he could out of anyone. To consider that he might threaten anyone who knew about his stealing from here, to make sure they kept quiet and didn't report his actions, is certainly a possibility."

"It is," Ashley agreed as they climbed into her car. "It's something we'll definitely need to dig deeper into to investigate. For all we know, it was just a rumor that was started by someone who just didn't like him. I mean, the fact that nobody reported him when it sounds like the rumor was pretty rampant, at least for a while, might suggest that there was nothing to it. We haven't yet heard of him having been actually involved in any kind of relationship with anyone. That doesn't mean he didn't use the same charm on the people who worked here, that he did online."

"Could have charmed someone and given them the wrong idea before rejecting their advances, or maybe stepped on the toes of another person, coming onto someone who was attached?" Tim pondered.

"Anything is possible," said Ashley. "If there's one thing this job has taught me over the years, it's that there is *nothing* that any human does to another, that is surprising anymore. People ... as much as I wish everyone would just be at peace with one another, that kind of world only lives in fiction."

"Such a negative view of the world, Ash!" Tim teased her before growing serious. "But I do understand what you're saying. That's the worst thing about this job - seeing almost daily just how horrible some people are."

CHAPTER 13

Back at the hotel, Ashley and Tim settled at the table in Tim's room, ready to study the new files they'd been provided access to.

"All of these are only about Lance Summers," Tim said when he saw the content. "It's not often that you and I are working on a case that centers around not one but two victims."

"True, but even though there does seem to be similarities between these deaths, we don't yet know if there is actually any connection," said Ashley. "Let's see what Mr Lance Summers might have done to deserve what's happened to him," Ashley said as she opened up her laptop.

"We only have some records of his online transactions," Tim said. "There are no dodgy looking transactions in these bank accounts, although tech have said there are more accounts that they're still waiting to receive records for. They also haven't got the phone records yet."

"Okay," said Ashley. "Best we do as we did with Bob Masters then. Let's delve into Summers' social media and see if this guy left any footprint of his existence there."

Searching the usual social media options, as well as running an image search using the victim photo that Pete Thoms had provided, both agents were surprised to find no online trace of the victim at all.

"That's odd," Tim said, thoughtful.

Ashley smiled at what she knew was an insinuation on his part.

"Odd?" she asked, grinning. "That he isn't in any of those sites you searched?"

"Yeah," Tim replied before realizing why she was smiling. "Yeah, I know. *You* aren't on any social media sites. But, Ash, most people are - well, most *normal* people anyway," he added, seizing the moment to tease her right back.

"I don't know what you're implying, Moore, but my life works just fine without being online all the time, looking at videos of kittens and puppies," she retorted, making him laugh out loud.

"Yeah, I know," Tim said before refocusing and growing serious again. "And you're right - not everyone *does* use social media. Hopefully, the tech guys will be able to provide us with some more useful information when they've completed all of their searches. While I concede that not everyone is in social media, there *was* a computer in his home, so there's a good chance he's been using that for something. Maybe it wasn't used for this purpose, but I'd bet that he was going online at some point for something, even if just for watching porn."

Ashley raised her eyebrows but didn't respond with words. She could have argued that not everyone looked at porn either, but she was happy to wait and see what came of their future findings from the Bureau's tech guys. In her opinion, they were amazing. If there was anything to find out, they'd find it.

CHAPTER 14

Hours later, Ash and Tim made their way to the North Road Fire Station once again.

"Hi," a firefighter called out on noticing Ashley as she and Tim entered the large building structure. "Can I help you?"

"Thanks, but we're just here to see your boss," Ashley replied, smiling at him.

"I can take you…" the man began to say.

"No need, but thanks," Ashley said. "We know the way."

As she and Tim continued on their way to the office of the station captain, Ashley caught the small smile on Tim's face. He was itching to tease her yet again about some guy liking the look of her, and she could tell.

"Don't even think it, Moore," she said, making him laugh. No more needed to be said on that subject.

"I was just about to give you guys a call," Captain John Rogers called out to them as they entered. "Come through."

Without words, Ashley and Tim walked to where the fire department captain stood. Once seated inside his office again, they waited.

"You've heard about this second fire?" John asked and saw each agent nod.

"Sergeant Thoms called us earlier, after the fire had been put out and the investigators were doing their search and assessment," Ashley replied. "You don't attend scenes yourself, Captain?" she asked, noting she'd not seen him there, but not sure if he would be offended in any way by the question.

"Not too often these days," John replied. "For the most part, my active days as a firefighter are over. Twenty years of doing that full-time was more than enough for this old body," he said. "These days, I coordinate the crews and handle all of the paperwork. That's enough for me now."

Tim nodded while he kept observing the man before him. There was something not quite likable about John Rogers, but Tim didn't express that, or any concerns he might have been starting to have about the man they faced.

"But enough about me," John said, smiling in a surprising way at Ashley.

"Yes," Ashley said, having also noticed an odd vibe emanating toward her. "The victim - Lance Summers. Do you know anything about him? Or know him?"

"Nope," the captain replied, easing back in his chair in an almost defiant or defensive manner. It was a stark contrast to the relaxed vibe he'd given off only moments earlier. "Can't say I do - or did."

"The investigator report?" Tim began to ask.

"Not here yet," John replied. "Their in-depth report probably won't arrive till tomorrow. That particular crew are pretty fast with their investigating and reporting, especially when there's been a body found, but it would never be a same-day situation. I have, however, spoken to their crew leader briefly. He confirmed to me that one person was in the house at the time of the fire, and his first opinion was that the gas line had been cut in exactly the same way as the Masters fire."

"Who, exactly, would know how to do something

like that, do you think?" Tim asked.

"Cut a gas line?" John asked, not hiding a slight smirk. "Anyone, I guess."

"Do you think this person would have to have some in-depth or trade knowledge about it though?" asked Ashley. "I mean, I would expect a gas leak in a home to maybe cause someone to go to sleep and not wake up. I wouldn't expect every instance of this kind of … arson, I guess? … to result in explosions like this."

"True," John said. "And you are right. Not all instances of leaking gas would result in this particular thing happening…"

"But in both of these cases, it has," Tim said. "Could that mean that someone knows this is what's going to happen?"

"It's possible," John replied as he shrugged his shoulders. "Hard to say, really, until you can speak to the perpetrator, and that's your job rather than mine."

"Have there been other instances of this kind of thing happening recently, Captain?" Ashley asked.

"No, none," the captain replied. "We attend our fair share of fires in homes around the area, but no, I haven't seen anything like this in my career with the fire department. Two homes go up in flame after a gas explosion? And within such a short amount of time? No, definitely not something usual around here."

"What about instances of gas lines appearing to have been cut, but didn't result in fire or explosion?" asked Ashley.

"Nothing like that has been reported to me, but if that had happened, it's possible the home owner would call someone other than the fire department," John said. "For reports on anything like that - something that didn't result in fire - you might need to check with the police department or the gas providers."

"Who, in your opinion, would have knowledge about how gas lines work, and how gas can be extra dangerous in various situations?" asked Tim.

"Or even, who would know how to do something like interfere with a residential gas supply, without causing any harm to themselves?" Ashley added.

"If you want my opinion - and I'm only guessing, mind you - you could be looking for someone … in a gas installation business maybe? They'd certainly be the most aware of how gas lines work, and what the dangers are when working around gas. Other than that, I'm not sure."

"Do you know of any particular gas providers here?" Tim asked but could sense the captain appearing to grow weary of answering their questions. It was an odd thing to see in the body language of someone who worked in a role dedicated to helping members of a community.

"No, but you'll find some in the telephone book," John replied, not hiding some curtness in his voice. "There are at least a couple in town."

"Alright," Ashley said as she also sensed a change in the manner and tone of the man before them. "Well, you have been very helpful, Captain. We'll leave you now, but if you could contact us when you have the full investigator report…"

"Of course. Like I say, they're usually pretty quick but it's unlikely to be today that it comes through. I'd expect to see it in the morning, at the earliest," both agents heard John say before he then appeared to see something far more important on his computer screen.

Without saying any more, Tim and Ashley walked out of the office and out of the station, both feeling like they'd been completely dismissed.

"He's an interesting bloke, isn't he," Tim said when they were settled into the car. "One minute, he seems friendly and eager to help us. The next..."

"Yeah, I'm not sure what's up with him," Ashley agreed as she heard Tim's words drift off. "Like you said, one minute he's one thing. The next, he's something entirely different. A bit too Jekyll and Hyde-ish for me!"

"Seems to like you more than me, too," Tim said, smirking. "Can't understand that."

Ashley chuckled. Even though they were on a serious mission, she did now and then appreciate her partner's effort to lighten the seriousness, at least for a moment.

"Maybe we should look into our fire station captain as well," she said after consideration. "Can't hurt to check him out."

"On it," Tim said as he pulled out his phone and fired through the request. "You really think he could be a suspect?"

"At this stage, *everyone's* a suspect."

CHAPTER 15

"That's three gas installation places I've got the addresses of, Ash," Tim said later, after having done some research. "Go and see each of them?"

"Absolutely," Ashley replied as she jumped up from the small table in her hotel room. "These guys should be able to shed some more light on what kind of person would have the knowledge to do something like this."

"They might also be unknowingly harboring a killer," Tim said before they left the room. "Or knowingly."

"That is entirely possible," Ashley acknowledged. "If not, though, I think it'll be good for us to gain a better understanding of how exactly gas explosions happen. I know we've read the report about the fire at Bob Masters' home, but it still seems odd to me that such a small thing, like a gas line being cut, could do so much damage."

"I think in his case, from what the report indicated, the gas had just been leaking for such a long time..." Tim started to say.

"Yeah, but then how did he not smell it when he entered that day?" asked Ashley. "I've never had gas in any place I've lived, but I've smelt it in other people's homes."

"You smelt it possibly because it wasn't a regular scent to you," said Tim as they approached Ashley's car. "Like with anything, someone who's around it every day might not be so sensitive to the smell of it."

"True," Ashley agreed when they'd climbed inside.

During the drive over to the premises of the first gas installation company, both agents were quiet. So far, it was only an initial first-impression assessment that had left the scene investigators to think that the fire at the home of Lance Summers might be due to the same situation as the one at the home of Bob Masters. It wasn't conclusive yet, but Ashley looked forward to reading the final report that would provide a solid conclusion to that belief.

"You know what I find odd about these two explosions happening?" she heard Tim ask, breaking her out of her thoughts.

"What?" she asked, prompting him to continue.

"They're both in this town," Tim replied, his voice betraying how curious he was about the aspect. "We had assumed that whoever killed Bob Masters might have been out of town - one of his online victims that he'd been leading on, making them think he was further away than he was."

"And now you're wondering if it's not one of those women?" Ashley asked.

"Yeah," said Tim. "Now I'm wondering if it's just someone in this town, and it's because of a completely different reason."

"Something that Bob Masters and Lance Summers were caught up in together…" Ashley pondered.

"Exactly," Tim replied as the car veered into a parking spot outside the first business.

"Well, let's see what these guys have to say, and what we can learn about gas explosions and fire in general," Ashley said as they climbed out of the car. "Maybe once we understand more about this way of killing someone, we'll see a wider possibility about who is behind this."

Walking inside the large garage area that housed one work van and many outer wall shelves holding all kinds of hoses and fittings, Ashley and Tim were greeted by a young man.

"Can I help you?" he asked when they entered.

"We hope so," Ashley said. "We're hoping to talk to whoever is in charge here."

Although the young man looked nervous as soon as she spoke, she immediately then saw him wipe his hands on his work trousers before plastering a smile on his face.

"Yeah, my boss is this way," he finally said, as if whatever had made him visibly nervous had never been a big deal at all.

Tim and Ashley glanced at each other briefly before following the young man through two doors, until they were standing inside a small office.

"Boss, these two people are wanting to speak to you," the young man said before once again standing still, as if about to get told off for something.

"Thanks, Tom," the man behind the desk said, not bothering to stand to greet the agents. "Off you go!" he added, prompting the young man to leave the room. "What can I do for you folks?" he asked, finally addressing Tim and Ashley.

"We're Special Agents Power and Moore, from the Bureau of Investigation," Ashley said. "We're hoping you might be able to help us in our investigation into two gas explosions that have happened near here recently."

The man studied both agents for a long while before leaning forward, placing his arms on his desk, and replying.

"Special Agents? Bureau of Investigation?" he asked and saw Tim and Ashley nod. "What's this really about?"

"Two people have been killed with what we think might have been the same method," Tim said. "Two houses, two explosions, and two bodies."

"And you think ... *I* have something to do with this?" the man asked, surprising both agents.

"Actually, we were hoping we could just get your insight into gas lines - how they could be cut, what they could be cut with, and how that could result in an explosion," Tim replied.

Once again, the man took his time to look at each of the agents before he answered.

"Depends on the situation," he said. "Residential home?" he asked and saw Ashley and Tim nod. "Well, then it depends on whether it's a gas line hooked up to a major gas supply, or if it's a gas supply coming from individual tanks."

"Is ... do people in homes around here have that option?" Tim asked.

"They do," the man replied, nodding. "This town was built with gas feeding into each property, but when the gas prices skyrocketed two decades ago, some people decided to stop using gas altogether, so had their lines disconnected. If someone's purchased any of those homes since then, and then decided they do want gas after all, nowadays it's easier to just have tanks installed, and replaced as they need them."

"How does that system work?" asked Ashley.

"We have the large tanks here," the man said. "Some folks are on a regular changeover plan, so we go to their homes on a set day every month or two, depending on what they've signed up for, and we swap the empty tanks for full ones. Other people are set up to just call us when one of their tanks is empty. With that system, we go and swap the empty tank out as required. Easy enough system that, these days, more and more people seem to prefer rather than paying for an ongoing connection all the time."

"And either of these could result in an explosion?" Ashley asked, aware that even though the man before them knew what they wanted to know, he didn't appear in any way forthright in offering information.

"Gas can be a fickle thing," he finally replied. "Generally, these days, gas explosions in private homes are less common - and not even particularly likely. I'm guessing you've read some kind of report that details what happened in these cases that you're looking into."

"Yes," Ashley said. "We do know that both were homes with an established gas line."

"Right," the man said. "I don't see how I can help you with that."

"Would someone need to be experienced in knowing about, or working around, gas lines, to know how to cut one safely?" Tim asked, experiencing a growing dislike for the person in front of them.

"*Should* they? Yes," the man replied. "But do they *need* to, just to cut a line? No. Anyone with a box cutter could cut through one of those lines. Not straight away, mind you. Over the years, the lines have been reinforced to stop general wear and tear happening, which in turn makes it harder to simply cut through the tubing. If someone did that, either they have a lot of patience, or they've used some kind of tool - maybe some kind of power saw, I'm guessing. Is that what's happened in these cases?"

"We're still investigating, but the lines were definitely cut," Tim said. "That much, we know for certain."

"Then it's probably someone who knows what they're doing," said the man. "You thinking it's someone who works here?"

"So far, we're exploring all avenues, so haven't

ruled any possibility out," Ashley replied. "But of course, we are allowing for the possibility that it could be a gas worker..."

"None of my workers would do something like that," the man said, his tone returning to its initial unfriendly state. "These guys are all good workers. Some of them are young, but none of them are any trouble. If you ask me what kind of person you could be looking for, yes, it might be someone who knows about gas, but both instances resulted in explosions?"

"Yes, one small enough to start a fire and result in a death, but most of the home is still standing," said Tim. "The other one resulted in a pretty large mess of an explosion."

"Sounds like you're after someone who likes that then," the man said before providing his final summary. "You're looking for someone who likes explosions. If that wasn't what they were hoping for, they could have killed someone another way, right?"

"We can't yet know what the intention of the ... arsonist ... was," Ashley said. "Would it be possible to tamper with the gas line but *not* have it result in an explosion?"

"Of course," the man replied, smiling at her as if she was an absolute idiot. "I'm assuming these fires happened when the person inside lit a match..."

"We think so," said Tim, feeling particularly protective over Ashley, and not at all liking the way the man before them was looking at her. "The first victim appeared to have started to use his range."

"That'd do it," the man replied. "When the line was cut, it only would have allowed gas to enter the house. For the majority of instances, even that wouldn't do much since most homes have some form of ventilation happening, through uninsulated walls, or just gaps around doors or windows. If gas was leaking into an enclosed space, it should have been able to leak *out* once a door or window was opened, reducing the chances of any explosion, even if a match was struck. It was a big explosion, you say?"

"Yes," Tim replied. "One was."

"Then that house must have not only had gas leaking into it over a prolonged period of time, but it must have been pretty air tight," the man said.

"And someone would be able to *smell* the gas?" Ashley asked.

"If it was from our supply, yes," the man replied. "The gas we sell is purposely scented strong enough to be able to be easily smelt. If it built up in a confined area, I can't see how the presence of it could have been missed."

"That's not the case with all gas provided to homes?" asked Tim.

"No," the man said. "Gas, in its natural form, is quite mild. I mean, I would expect most people would still notice it, at least a little, but if you're around it all the time, it can be subtle enough to just get used to. If someone was experiencing a leak over a long period of time, they literally might have grown used to the smell of it without even knowing."

"But that would mean ... someone had a small leak, and then what? It got bigger?" Tim asked, feeling a little like they were getting nowhere with their questioning.

"That's a possibility," the man answered as he nodded. "That would mean two visits to the gas line, though. You guys will have a better idea than me about the minds of people who do stupid things." He paused for a long while, appearing to think about possibilities. "Look, all I can tell you for sure is that my crew here are a good lot," he said. "I don't think any of them would do anything to harm anyone.

They're all safety conscious on the job, and none of them … *none* of them have the kind of personality that would make me think they'd want to hurt someone. And if you're talking about what I think you're talking about - someone went to a residential home and deliberately cut a gas line with the intention of hurting or killing someone - no, none of this lot would do that. I just can't believe that."

Ashley watched the man's face as he spoke. So far, he hadn't offered his name, or bothered to move at all from the desk he'd been sitting at when Ashley and Tim had entered his office. It was a weird way to act, in Ashley's opinion, but throughout her career with the bureau she'd learned that there were lots of different kinds of people, and many of them were never friendly towards anyone in law enforcement.

"Alright, well I think that's all we need to ask for now," Tim said, wondering if the man before them would offer anything more useful. When nothing came, Tim stood up. "Thank you, Mr…" he said, purposely holding out his hand for a handshake.

Finally, as she stood, Ashley saw the man stand and hold out his hand, placing it into Tim's.

"Sanderson," he said. "Evan Sanderson."

"Thank you, Mr Sanderson," Ashley said. "You've given us much to think about."

Tim and Ashley were about to leave the office when they heard the man call out one more time.

"Explosions," he said, prompting Ashley and Tim to both stop in their steps, and turn to face him. "Try looking for someone who has some weird obsession with explosions or fires. As weird as they are, those people exist - but they ain't here."

Hearing the finality in his voice, both agents smiled at him and silently left the office.

As they made their way back to the car, both

noticed the same young man in the large garage area looking at them. For a moment, Ashley wondered if he was going to approach them and say something. Another moment later, she realized he wasn't. Instead of moving towards them, he abruptly appeared to change his mind, turning instead to simply present his back to them.

"Well, that was … interesting," Tim said once they were settled into the car once again. "He's not exactly the most welcoming guy, is he, that Mr Sanderson."

"No, not at all," Ashley agreed. "But at least we learned a little about how the gas gets to the homes in this area."

"Yeah, but does it help us at all?" Tim asked.

"Well, he did say that 'a' - the gas that goes to homes via this place is purposely scented so that nobody should be able to not notice it, and 'b' - that someone might have needed to visit the homes twice to be able to let the gas build up in a way that wasn't necessarily noticed by the victims," Ashley said as she fastened her seatbelt and turned to face Tim. "Not much to go on, granted, but maybe it'll prove useful once we get more information about this latest victim."

"True," said Tim. "I'm now wondering if we should talk to John Rogers again. Maybe he knows of someone who's got some fascination with explosions."

"Good idea," Ashley said as she started the engine. "It's certainly a line of enquiry worth pursuing, Partner!"

CHAPTER 16

"Twice in one day," Captain John Rogers said when he saw Tim and Ashley enter his office again. "To what do I owe this pleasure? The scene investigation report for the Summers home isn't in yet."

"Oh, no, we know that won't be back today, Captain," Ashley said. "We'd like to ask if you know of anyone who might have shown a particular interest in these two fires - or explosions."

Both agents watched the expression on John's face once again change from that of welcoming, to something quite different.

"On my crew, do you mean?" he finally asked.

"No, not specifically," Tim replied as he sat down. "Perhaps you or your crew noticed someone - anyone - around the scenes of the fires when you've attended them. Someone who seemed overly excited by what was happening?"

John nodded but took his time before he replied.

"The first scene, my guys were pushed to try and get the fire under control," he said. "There's no way any of them would have had time to see what was happening in the crowd that assembled to watch the Masters home go up in flames. As for the second one - the Summers home - well, you two were there fairly shortly after it happened. I was there for a while but didn't notice anyone who looked suspicious. Did you?"

Ashley felt a sting at the question being thrown

back at her and Tim. Pushing it aside, she moved forward in her questioning.

"What about your crew?" she dared to ask.

"What about them?" John responded.

"Is anyone among your staff particularly interested in these kinds of fires?" Tim asked.

"The kind of fires that ... *kill* people?" asked John before abruptly shaking his head. "No, none of my guys are that way inclined. There's nobody here who I've ever seen get excited or anything else over a fire. When they're called to a scene, they get on with the job of securing it to make sure everyone is safe, and making sure the fire is properly out. Nobody in this station would be behind *starting* fires, if that's what you're insinuating."

"We aren't insinuating anything, Captain," Ashley said quietly in an attempt to calm down the man before her. She had a job to do, but she could understand how and why he'd gone from appearing friendly, to being someone who was willing to stand up and fight for his people. "It's our job to weigh up all possibilities."

"Well, looking at fire fighters isn't one of those possibilities!" John exclaimed. "I suggested you go and talk to the gas companies in town."

"And we have done that," Ashley said, continuing to keep her voice steady and unaffected by the unfriendly tone coming back at her. "Our questions are only part of our general enquiry. I'm sure you're aware that we have to consider and follow up all possibilities. Although Bob Masters didn't appear to have any family remaining, he still deserves the truth to be found, no matter where that lies."

She watched as John seemed to try to calm down before he responded to her words with his own.

"Yes, of course," he said. "But let me be clear.

Nobody in this station has ever shown any particular desire or fascination with the fires we attend. Honestly, in my long career in firefighting, I have seen people like that - the kind of people who were a bit too enthusiastic about the scenes we attended. Nobody like that is currently on this team."

"Currently?" Tim asked, curious about the statement. "When you say you have seen people like that in firefighting before, are these people who are still in the area?"

"Some," John acknowledged. "But they're my age, or even older."

"Was someone you know of dismissed from the fire service *because* of their actions - or reactions - to fires?" Ashley asked, intrigued about where the discussion had turned.

It seemed a long time before John replied. When he did, his face revealed dismay.

"Yes," he said. "My brother-in-law. Five years ago. He served here for two years, during which time there was a bout of six fires, all of which were similar in nature, as far as the scene investigators were concerned."

"And ... people died in the fires?" Ashley asked, wondering why none of what she was hearing had been mentioned previously.

"No," John said. "No, those instances weren't the same as the Masters and Summers fires. My brother-in-law was just a firefighter who liked fire. After the police started looking into what looked like a string of arson attacks, they pinpointed who it was. But he didn't have any wish to hurt people. Turned out he thought he was *helping* them," he added as he scoffed.

"How so?" asked Tim.

"It was for people he'd heard were having a hard time financially," John said. "After he made sure they had full house insurance and they were out of their homes, he started the fires so those people could claim back what they'd lost, and more."

Ashley remained quiet as she processed the news.

"What happened to him after he was identified as the perpetrator?" she asked.

"Went to prison, of course," John replied. "Served two years and then got out. My sister divorced him and took the kids up north. Hasn't heard from him since."

"Do you think there's a possibility he's back?" asked Tim.

"Whether he is or he isn't, I..." John started to reply before appearing to need to really take some time to consider the question. "I can't see it being him who's causing these happenings. Like I said, in his mind he was helping people, not hurting them. He wasn't - isn't - a killer. Plus, he liked *fires*. He wasn't into setting up houses to explode. No. Of course I could be wrong, but I don't think I am. He isn't your suspect."

Quietly wondering to himself why nobody had mentioned the arson attacks previously, Tim processed what the Captain had told them, and then filed it away in his mind.

"Just so we can absolutely rule him out, what is your brother-in-law's name?" Ashley asked.

"It's not..." John began to insist, before he showed signs of acceptance that he wouldn't be able to stop the agents from seeking whatever they wanted to find out. "Tony ... Tony Forbes."

"Thank you," Tim said as he saw Ashley stand. "We'll chat again when the scene report comes through."

"Of course," John replied, remaining where he was. Whatever emotions the discussion had summoned in him, Ashley and Tim could both see he was in pain at that moment.

Neither agent said anything more as they made their exit.

CHAPTER 17

"Interesting conversation, that one," Tim said as they began their journey back to the hotel.

"Yeah, although I'm left wondering why neither he nor Sergeant Thoms mentioned that whole fire arson situation to us before," Ashley said. "Surely either of them must have thought about it when this second fire happened."

"Yeah, maybe," said Tim. "Although, as John said, his brother-in-law seemed to be on a mission to help people, as misguided as that might seem to you and me. If John was telling the truth about the lengths Tony went to before he was caught, it doesn't really fit with what's happening here. Even though we know that people escalate in their behaviors when it comes to arson and the like, to go from trying to help people to trying to kill them is a bit of a stretch."

"True," Ashley agreed. "We should look into where he is though. If he's anywhere in the area at the moment, we might need to seek him out and talk to him. It could be that his enthusiasm has escalated to wanting to watch explosions happen that result in fire, and the two situations producing victims wasn't intended."

"True. I'll send through the request now," Tim said before his phone vibrated in his pocket. "Oh, Tech have just sent through docs about Lance Summers as well."

"Great," Ashley replied as she pulled into the hotel

carpark. "Perfect timing."

Inside her hotel room, she watched Tim set up his laptop. Once ready, both sat and studied what was presented before them.

"Looks like Mr Summers has got something in common with Bob Masters after all," Ashley said.

"They were both spending time online, trying to use women," Tim agreed as he read the document on the screen. "But look at this, Ash," he said as he pointed to one detail. "Some of these messages indicate he did actually meet these women in person."

"Different from Bob Masters in that regard then," said Ashley. "Yeah, you're right. There's plenty here to indicate he met a few women in real life."

"Seven names that I can see, looking at this list," Tim agreed. "All quite young…"

"He was thirty," Ashley remembered.

"And these women look … yeah, they all look like they're in their twenties," said Tim.

"Young and naive," Ashley mumbled to herself.

"You don't have to be young to be naïve, Ash," Tim said, chuckling as he chastised her for saying something that made her seem ageist. "Not all young people are immature, and not all older people are wise!"

"That is very true!" Ashley agreed. "Let's look closer at his text message history."

Heads together, both agents took their time to read through every message that had been sent and received by Lance Summers over the previous three months.

"He's so much like Bob Masters in his approach to these women," Ashley said after a long while. "These guys sure know how to charm women - enough for me to wonder why they use online methods to do this at all. If they're so charming, couldn't they have anyone they wanted? Why do things this way, and live a life mostly online?"

"Maybe they didn't want to be attached," Tim replied as he shrugged his shoulders. "Being single isn't all that bad," he added, grinning at Ashley.

"Oh, I know that!" Ashley exclaimed. "But … okay, so, Bob Masters was asking women for money. He'd charm them, and then, once he felt he'd secured their affection and trust, he'd ask them to make a cash deposit into his bank account, after which he'd quietly start extracting himself from replying to their messages. As far as we can tell from what we read of his online antics, he never had any intention of actually meeting any of them."

"Agreed," Tim said in response. "Bob Masters wasn't looking to meet anyone in person at all. He wanted to use women for cash, and that's what he did, without even having to set foot outside of his home if he didn't want to."

"Right," Ashley replied. "But this guy - Lance - he seems to have met all of these women. He's followed a similar path as far as finding targets goes, but then he's taken it one step further and actually met them in person. He's shown himself to be the real person they think he is, both with what he looks like compared to his photos, and what kind of nature he has."

"Yeah, but he still ripped them off, by the looks of it," said Tim. "Look at these messages. They follow a similar path - this guy charms these women, he does meet them, but after he gets something out of them, he starts to withdraw, as if they're no use to him anymore."

"Some people could describe that as every adult on the planet," Ashley said as she quietly chuckled. "What did he get though? Are his bank account records here somewhere? Was he after cash as well?"

"We haven't got the bank statements yet," said Tim after double checking his email contents. "But some of these messages make it seem like he was getting the women to hotel rooms…"

"Using them for sex then…" Ashley surmised.

"Maybe, primarily, but look at the wording of some of these," said Tim, pointing to the screen again. "I'm wondering if he got a whole lot more from these women."

"This statement of phone activity shows the numbers of the women he was in contact with," said Ashley. "Any overlap with the list of women Bob was messaging?"

"Bob kept almost all of his messaging to inside the dating site app or inside his social media accounts," said Tim. "But at a glance … no, there are no numbers that were recently used by Bob, that were also recently used by Lance."

"Okay, well Tech have provided us with the names and possible addresses of these seven women," Ashley said. "They're all in this neighboring town so let's call it a night and head out in the morning to see if we can talk to any of them."

"Or we could just call them," Tim cheekily suggested, expecting the eye roll that he did then receive from Ashley. "I mean, we have their numbers."

"You know me, Moore," Ashley retorted. "I prefer to ask questions face to face. We always see far more than we hear!"

"Yep," Tim agreed, gaining joy from yet again getting a satisfactory response from his work partner. "I'll leave you in peace, then, and see you in the morning. Six-thirty for breakfast?"

"As always," Ashley replied before closing and double locking her door. She'd been feeling like they were reaching out and seeking lots of different angles without any success in finding any real connections. Finally, she felt like they might be on some sort of path to finding out what had been going on. It wasn't much to go on yet, but that was normal for them.

Sometimes she felt like they were frequently at crossroads when they embarked upon an investigation. Right in the center of those crossroads, they might remain for a long time or a short time. Either way, eventually they always began to move down one of the roads. Sometimes they'd keep going down that road, but there were plenty of times when they needed to double back to that center point again and try another road after all.

There was still much to learn, but possibilities had already opened up to them. That was more than enough to smile about as she lay down on her bed, then went through her usual mantras and routine to let the day's learnings slip away for at least a few hours. Soon enough, Special Agent Ashley Power was fast asleep.

CHAPTER 18

"Good morning," Tim greeted Ashley as he saw her closing her hotel door upon his approach along the corridor the following morning.

"Hey," Ashley greeted him. "Sleep well?"

"Yep, pretty comfy bed so can't complain," Tim replied, grinning.

"Ready for food?" asked Ashley, knowing he always seemed to want to eat.

"You know it!" Tim responded as they began their walk to the breakfast room.

After being greeted and seated, and giving their orders, both agents refocused.

"So where are we at?" Ashley asked him. "We know that both of our victims were using women, and doing so through online means. It's not much to go on, and not anything to match them together."

"No, but more documents came in overnight," Tim said. "The bank accounts of Summers show no deposits other than his regular pay, so I don't think he was asking for money, or being paid it by the women he was charming online."

"Right," said Ashley. "Or if he was, he was being careful to not have any of them give him the money by deposit into his account."

"Yes, that is true," Tim said. "There is always the possibility that he was getting money out of them, but in the form of cash - especially since we know that he met at least some of his targets in person."

"True, but seeing he had no deposits into his bank account from any of these women does rule out that connection between Masters and Summers then," said Ashley before noticing how her partner was looking at her. "I can see by your expression that there's something more you haven't told me yet. Come on, Moore. Out with it."

"Well, Lance Summers *was* in the same dating site as Bob Masters - Date Today," Tim replied. "Could that be a coincidence? It *is* something that they were both doing."

"Hmm, okay," Ashley said. "It's not a great link though, is it. I mean, millions of people must be on those sites. The odds are high that quite a few of any town or city will be."

"That's true," said Tim. "But what if … and it's a long shot … what if someone working for that dating site itself was doing this?"

"Tim, that's way outside the realm of even being a long shot," Ashley said, surprised by where his thinking had gone. "Why … *how* … would anyone do that anyway? Even if it was some kind of administrator who did happen to read some messages, and not like what they read - how are they going to find out where these guys live?"

"Administrators would have easy access to where people are," Tim replied. "They are the exact people who can see through IP addresses, where the user is."

"They can see the region, or even immediate area, but see *exactly* where they are?" Ashley asked. "Are you sure?"

"I'll have to ask the Tech team about that, sure, but let's say that the dating site administrator *can* see those details of their users," Tim suggested. "They read something they don't like. They follow up to find out where that user is…"

"And then jump on a plane to go and kill the user?" Ashley asked. As farfetched as it sounded, she knew it was something they'd need to look into. People had killed for far less than seeing how badly some women were treated. "I'm not sure about this one, Tim, but yes, get the team to delve further into whoever is behind the dating app itself. Who knows - maybe they will find something worth investigating there. In the meantime, we know of seven women who met Lance Summers in person. That's more than we had with Mr Masters. Let's eat up and then go see what these women have to say."

As their meals were placed in front of them, Tim grinned at her. Whatever avenue they ever went down when investigating a case, he loved that they were both on the same path of believing that every possibility had to be looked at - even the ones that seemed incredibly unlikely.

CHAPTER 19

"At least all of these women are within a relatively close distance from one another," Ashley said as they entered the neighboring town.

"None of them live in the same town as where Summers lived though," said Tim.

"Maybe that was the attraction for him," Ashley said as Tim glanced at her. "Close enough for him to easily get to the women when he wanted to see them. Far enough away that they couldn't smother him or his efforts to have multiple women that he was using."

Pulling up to the home of the first woman, they knocked but could see nobody was home. The same was true of the second woman. Approaching the home of the third on the list, however, they were in luck.

"Ms Sanders?" Ashley called out to a woman who was kneeling on the ground, appearing to be doing some weeding of her front yard.

"Yes," the woman replied. "Can I help you?"

"I'm Special Agent Ashley Power, and this is Special Agent Tim Moore," Ashley replied. "We're with the Bureau of Investigation."

"Yes? What's this about?" the woman asked as she stood and approached the agents.

"We'd like to ask you about a gentleman of the name Lance Summers," Ashley asked. Straight away, she found a hand on her elbow, guiding her closer to the footpath.

"I can't talk about that here," the woman said in a

hushed tone. "I can meet you in town - at the Stray Cat Café? Twenty minutes?"

Ashley could see mild panic on the woman's face. It was easy to assume one thing, but she knew she needed to hear whatever the woman could tell them.

"We can do that if it is better for you..."

"Yes!" the woman exclaimed. "Please leave, but I will be there. If not twenty minutes, I will be close. Wait for me."

Ashley nodded and turned to walk with Tim back to the car. Once seated inside, they saw the woman quickly pick up her gardening items and then walk around the side of the house, disappearing from their view.

"Affair?" Tim asked.

"That's my guess too," said Ashley. "Or she knows something and she's about to do a runner."

"Let's give her the benefit of the doubt," Tim said. "She honestly looked worried about something, and we know this is definitely her home. If she doesn't turn up at the café, we can come back."

It was always a long shot, trusting if someone they wanted to question was going to turn up where and when they'd stated they would. With some people, Ashley felt in her gut that they wouldn't be trustworthy, and had no intention of turning up. She didn't sense that with the woman she'd just spoken to.

"Okay, let's go and find this place," she said before they began their journey. "I hope it's not literally filled with stray cats."

The comment made Tim chuckle. Even though he felt like he'd gotten to know Ashley pretty well over their time working cases together, she could still sometimes surprise him by saying something he'd never expect to hear come from her mouth.

CHAPTER 20

"Thank you for agreeing to meet me here," Polly Sanders said quietly as she approached the table where the two agents sat. Sitting down, she took her time to breathe deeply until she looked far more relaxed.

"You do know Lance Summers then?" Tim asked when he sensed the woman was at ease.

"Yes," Polly said. "I … there's no way to say this without sounding like a … a *bad* wife, I guess. Yes, I was in a dating site, looking for … something else … and he messaged me. He looked tidy enough in his photos so we started chatting. He seemed nice … *then*."

"What happened after you started chatting?" asked Tim. "Did he hurt you?"

"No. Yes. I don't know," Polly replied. "We chatted for a few weeks, and then he started to suggest that we meet up. It wasn't a surprise to me, and to be honest, I got married just too young. I was feeling like I was overwhelmed, trying to do the grown up thing of being a wife and potential mother. Chatting online, and then meeting someone new in person - well … it felt … *I* felt young again."

Tim held his tongue at the comment. The woman in front of them was only in her twenties. In his eyes, she was still very young. Obviously, in her own, she wasn't.

"So, anyway, we met up one day at the local

beach," Polly continued. "We talked, we laughed, and then he suggested we meet up at a hotel one day when it suited me. I mean, I guess it was what I was really looking for. I just hadn't wanted to admit it."

"So you did meet him at a hotel?" Ashley asked and saw the woman nod. "On that first day?"

"Oh, no," Polly replied. "No, we met a few times in public first. It was probably - oh, I don't know - maybe the fourth time, that he suggested the hotel meet up. He was nice about it - well, I *thought* he was being nice about it - leaving it up to me to choose the date that suited, and the hotel that suited, and to just let me organize everything. He left it all to me, and said he would happily meet up with me once I gave him the details."

"So you arranged a day to meet up and then went to a hotel…" Tim prompted her to continue.

"Yes, at that point I was thankful that he was letting me take control of everything," Polly said. "It meant I could take my time and really think about it. I guess I should have felt guilty about what I was planning to do behind my husband's back, but at the time, I didn't. I was selfish, and only thinking of myself."

Ashley and Tim watched a diverse range of expressions flow over the woman's face as she appeared to be deep in thought about something.

"Yeah, so anyway, we met at the hotel," she finally continued. "Don't get me wrong - everything about meeting Lance at that hotel was good. He didn't rush me to do anything physical. He was understanding, and patient, and … he was everything that any woman could want for a … a situation like that."

"Meeting a lover," Tim suggested and saw her nod as she blushed.

"Yes," she said. "We had that afternoon together,

and I was so happy when I left there that I instantly booked another room for a few days later."

"And you met him again that second time?" asked Ashley.

"Yes, and again it was wonderful," Polly replied, smiling a little before the smile left her face.

"I'm sensing something wasn't quite so wonderful, Polly," Ashley suggested.

"At the hotel, everything *seemed* good," Polly said. "It was after that second time, when I looked at the bank statement of the credit card that I'd used, that I realized something wasn't all that wonderful after all. The cost of the room should have only been a hundred and fifty. The entire charge for the room was two *thousand*. Of course, I thought it must be a mistake so I went into the hotel and took my bank statement with me. Between the hotel manager, the hotel security footage, and me, it was established that during a very short time frame - I think only long enough for me to go and have a bath - Lance had ordered an extravagant amount of all sorts of things that were available for purchase at the hotel - food, giant bottles of the most expensive champagne, the expensive bathrobes that the hotel sold. It seemed like anything that he could get and could charge to the room - to *me!* - he got. I mean, what was he going to use five expensive bathrobes *for*?!"

"But didn't you see the items when you got out of the bath?" asked Tim.

"No," Polly replied. "No, when the hotel manager and I looked at the security footage that showed the corridor and elevators of the hotel, and then looked at the records of calls made from the room to the departments Lance ordered the things from, it looked like he'd pre-ordered everything. At first, I couldn't see how such a coincidence could happen, but then I remembered that he'd been the one to suggest I go and take a long, hot bubble bath, and that he'd join me after a while. It was all orchestrated by him. He pre-ordered items to make sure they would be ready whenever he asked for them to be delivered. Then he got me out of the room long enough for him to be able to accept the items *and* take them to his car."

"And then he returned…" Ashley started to ask.

"Yes, he then returned and joined me in the bath, sweeping me away all over again," Polly said. "I had no idea he'd even left the room, let alone all that he'd done in that short amount of time."

"What happened after that?" Tim asked. "Did you see the balance of the cost of your stay when you checked out?"

"No," Polly replied, shaking her head. "No, Lance had mentioned how amazing it was that hotels these days let people do the express checkout, which means just putting your key card in one of those slots and literally walking out. He made it sound like the greatest of ideas, not having to stand at the counter, waiting for a statement to be printed, like we used to have to do. What an idiot I was…"

"Not an idiot at all, Polly," Ashley said, sensing the deep regret emanating from the woman speaking. "Please continue."

"Once I saw the bank statement a few weeks later and spoke to the hotel, and I knew what he'd done, I messaged him to ask him why he'd done it," Polly said. "When he didn't reply, I knew I'd been had. I mean, I'd expected I was being used for sex, but it hadn't even occurred to me that he was using me to get whatever he could out of me financially on those two afternoons. He'd bought all of those things - I'm assuming to sell - and he'd also cleaned out the mini bar in the room. I was such a fool! No wonder he wanted me to book everything - it wasn't so that I could decide everything that worked for me. It was so that it would be my card that was charged for anything and everything associated with that time, and so that he couldn't be associated or held responsible for any of it!"

"Did you go to the police when you realized what had happened? What he'd done to you?" Tim asked.

"No. It was my own fault," Polly said. "I was stupid. And to be honest, I actually ended up assuming that he wasn't who he said he was. When I realized how he'd gotten away with so much, I expected that he hadn't used his real name, so what would have been the point of reporting it anyway? I was just an idiot."

"No, Polly. He stole from you," Ashley said. "That's not stupidity on your part. That's deception in his."

"Thank you, but I do take full responsibility for it," Polly insisted. "I was cheating on my husband. I did something I shouldn't have been doing, and I was made to pay for that."

"And your husband?" Tim asked.

"Knows nothing," said Polly. "We keep separate finances so he wouldn't have seen the way my bank account went from healthy to almost nothing. No, he doesn't need to know about any of this. He's a good man. I was the one who screwed up."

"Does anyone know about your affair then, Polly?" Ashley asked. "Did you tell anyone?"

"Not really. It's not something one would openly discuss with just anyone," Polly replied. "I told my sister and my closest few friends - only the ones I trusted would never tell anyone else. They were good, and so supportive. They told me it wasn't my fault too, but I still can't quite believe that. I'm just glad that me telling my friends hasn't resulted in them walking away from our friendships," she added before pausing for a long while. "Anyway, I tried a few times to get in contact with him, but he was already gone. There was never any reply to my messages, so that chapter is over with. I was stupid, and I now have to live with that, but it also taught me a lot. Trust nobody! That's the way to go!"

After appearing to ponder something for a long time, she looked up, glancing from one agent to the other.

"But you came looking for me, and you're asking about him, so you obviously know that I used to chat to him," she said. "Why are you wanting to talk to me? Has someone laid a complaint about him? Did he do this to other women?"

"Mr Summers is dead," Tim said while watching to see the resulting expression on Polly's face.

"What?" Polly asked.

"We're investigating his death," said Ashley. "How long has it been since you were in contact with him?"

"Oh … um … maybe two months?" Polly replied.

"And you never knew where he lived?" Ashley asked but saw the woman shake her head.

"No. Like I said, we only met in public places at first, and then at the hotel twice," said Polly. "I had no idea which part of town he lived in. He never talked about anything to do with his life - no work talk or anything. In hindsight, I can see that he had a remarkable way of keeping a conversation flowing for ages, asking lots of questions about me, while never actually *saying* much at all."

"And you're sure your husband had no idea about any of this?" asked Tim.

Polly looked horrified at the question that seemed to lie behind the one that had been asked.

"No!" she said. "And even if he had somehow found out about it, he wouldn't … no, if he'd found out, it would've been *me* he'd be angry with. But no, he knows nothing. I refuse to believe he could know, or that he could hurt someone if he had found out."

"Okay," Ashley said, sensing panic returning to the woman again. "You've been very helpful, Polly. Thank you for agreeing to talk to us."

"I … I don't know what to think, now that you've said he's dead," Polly said as if she was in a mild state of shock. "Do you think his death has something to do with someone like me? *Has* he done this to other people?"

"At this stage, we don't know, but we're investigating all avenues to try and find out what's happened," Ashley replied.

"A part of me … it sounds horrid, I'm sure, but a part of me hopes there are other women out there that he's done this to," Polly said. "I don't … I don't want to be the only one that was taken in by him."

"And you might not be," Ashley reassured her. "People who do things like this usually do go and do them to as many people as they can."

"Before someone makes them pay," Polly mumbled.

It was a comment that Ashley and Tim both took note of but decided to not question at that moment.

"Well, thank you," Ashley said as she and Tim stood. "If you think of anything else, will you call us?" she asked as she handed Polly a card with her contact details.

"I don't think there's anything more I can tell you, but yes, if I do think of something, I'll be sure to let you know," Polly said, remaining in her seat and refocusing on the cup of coffee in front of her.

Ashley and Tim said nothing more, instead leaving

the young woman to her thoughts as the two agents walked out and into the sunshine.

CHAPTER 21

"Polly Sanders didn't appear to be aware that Summers didn't live in her town," Tim said as he and Ashley began their journey back to their hotel. In the time since their meeting with Polly, they'd talked to four other women. All had told similar stories to Polly's.

"No, none of them seemed to mention that," Ashley said. "They all spoke as if they thought he was in the same town as them. It's weird, like he purposely targeted them because of their close vicinity to each other."

"And their distance from his own town," Tim added. "So we know that at least five of the women that Summers was chatting up, he managed to get into a lush hotel room…"

"At their expense," Ashley added.

"Yes, at their expense," Tim agreed. "Got them in there, got them to have a few hours of fun with him, then managed to coordinate every one of them to have a bath at a specific time, and for long enough so that he could have loads of expensive things delivered to the room, take the items out to his car, and be back to have a bath and more sex with these women without them having known he'd ever left."

"That seems like a pretty good summation there, Partner," Ashley said.

"What a plan!" Tim said in disbelief. "He must have had some kind of strategic brilliance or something, surely. What are the chances that such an exact plan would play out as easily as it seemed to, for every woman he tried it on?"

"It does seem pretty lucky on his part," Ashley agreed. "Then again, I guess with the right targets - women who feel lonely, or seem to have something missing in their lives, and feel like they need some physical attention, maybe they got from him what they were seeking."

"Ash! They obviously weren't seeking a huge *credit card bill* when they agreed to meet this guy!" Tim replied, the passion in his voice perfectly reflecting his views on how much better than that all women should be treated.

"True," said Ashley. "What we have to work out is whether someone knew what he was doing, or his death has nothing to do with this at all."

"Well, there is the connection between the *actions* of Masters and Summers - they were both actively finding and using women as targets for whatever scams they were doing - cash or freebies," Tim said as he pulled out his phone. "What we haven't explored properly yet is whether there was ever any contact between Summers and Masters. We don't know yet that they didn't know each other…"

"You think they might have been working together on something based around ripping women off?" Ashley asked. "Catfishing ring, or something like that?"

"It's an intriguing thought," Tim said. "I've heard of that kind of thing happening, where entire businesses are built up for the sole purpose of finding rich targets who'll pay money to whoever they think is behind the screen. Those scams usually end up being in places like Nigeria though. We know that Summers and Masters aren't there!"

"True, but that doesn't mean they weren't both part of a similar thing happening here," said Ashley. "You send through a request for analysis of the two of them being in contact?"

"Yep, it's done," Tim confirmed. "We didn't see any connection in the phone records we've already looked at, but if something connected them, the contact about it might be much further back."

"Interesting that both of these men only seemed to have contacted women too," Ashley pondered. "If someone was going to do a full-on scam like that, wouldn't they try and scam everyone, regardless of age or gender? I mean, even if they weren't gay, why not pretend to be women and attract straight guys, or pretend to be a gay guy, attracting gay guys? That would spread the possibility of income."

"Yeah, that would have worked okay for Bob Masters, since he never actually met anyone in person," Tim said. "Not such a wise idea for Summers though, unless he did like men and would have been happy to be in a hotel room with them."

"Which it doesn't sound like is the case, from what we've read and seen," Ashley agreed. "And I guess it's just easier pretending to be the gender and sexual orientation that you are. Plus, there are probably more than enough lonely women around for these guys to be kept busy doing what they're doing."

A few minutes later, Tim's phone buzzed in his pocket. After taking some time to read the content of the message that had come through, he turned to face Ashley.

"No records anywhere of any contact between Summers and Masters," he said. "The team have gone back about five years, for phone and digital contact. Nothing in there at all."

"That doesn't mean they weren't in contact," said

Ashley. "It just means they weren't in contact through those phones, or through usual means."

"That's true," said Tim as his phone buzzed again. "They've also said that the brother-in-law of John Rogers has been confirmed as being up north, not far from where his wife went with their kids. Local sheriff up there said one of his staff knows the guy and has confirmed he's been in the area pretty much every day since his release. It's possible he could have traveled this far, done a job, and then returned, but the sheriff doesn't think so. It's quite a distance north that they're at, and the guy's phone has been moving around in the same town constantly since he left."

"Okay, that's one possible suspect we can disregard then," said Ashley. "Even though he had some weird attraction to fire, and some weird belief that he was helping people, he hasn't connected directly to Masters or Summers at all anyway."

"Yeah, I think we can dismiss him completely as well," Tim agreed.

"Alright, well, where to now?" Ashley wondered as she thought about all that they'd learned. "We've got two male victims. Both have died in pretty much the same circumstances. Both were on dating sites…"

"Specifically Date Today," Tim added.

"Yes! Both were in Date Today," said Ashley. "And although their methods were different, both did, in one way or another, go out of their way to get something more lucrative than sex from the women they targeted."

"Agreed," said Tim as he watched her face.

Over the time that they'd worked together, he'd grown to admire much about Ashley. She was rarely humorous, but she had good skills in analysis, and a depth of wanting to work things out that Tim hadn't seen in other partners he'd had over his law enforcement career. For so many reasons, he was frequently grateful they'd been assigned together on so many cases.

"The question remains - if there is some connection between these guys, what is it?" Ashley asked, breaking Tim out of his thoughts.

"We're not there yet, Ash," he said, delivering her a confident grin. "But we will be soon enough!"

CHAPTER 22

"You're not going to believe this," Ashley's supervisor, Sarah, said to her over the phone an hour later. "I know you guys are already investigating two suspicious deaths down that way…"

As Ashley listened to the words and the tone of her supervisor, she felt a chill flow through her. It wasn't common for Sarah to contact her or Tim for idle chitchat while they were on a case. If she was calling, there was usually something very serious going on.

"What?" Ashley asked when she felt impatience hit.

"There's another one in the area," Sarah said.

"No, that can't be," Ashley said in disbelief. "You don't mean … another fire?"

"Yep," Sarah confirmed.

"Another *explosion*?"

"Yep."

"Another body?" Ashley asked in a whisper. Even the thought of it was horrifying to her. They hadn't made enough headway into the previous two deaths. That someone could keep doing what they were doing, right under their noses, made Ashley all the more sadder for the victims.

"Yep!" said Sarah. "It's a half hour drive away from where you are, but the same fire crew are on the scene."

"And the same scene investigators?" asked Ashley.

"I've just had confirmation that they're on their way

there now," said Sarah. "This fire happened about six hours ago, so it's cooling down now and the scene investigators will be moving in to do their thing when they get there." She paused a long while, expecting her agent to ask at least one question more. Hearing nothing more from Ashley at that moment, Sarah continued to speak. "Sorry. I know you've already got the other two…"

"No, that's fine, Sarah," said Ashley, forcing herself to move beyond the mild shock she felt from hearing the news. "Tim and I will get on it right away."

"Great," Sarah said. "I'm sending you all the details I have for now. I know this now means you'll be spanning three towns…"

"Yes, but that's no problem," said Ashley. "They're close to one another and, as you said, it's the same fire crews and scene investigators who are dealing with these. It makes sense that we keep assuming all of these fires are connected somehow."

"Okay," Sarah said. "I won't hold you up any longer."

"Thanks," Ashley said before hanging up.

Tim waited patiently to receive the news. He'd been watching his partner's face throughout almost of the entire call. It hadn't been difficult to see his partner's surprise at whatever news she'd just received.

"You're not going to believe this," Ashley finally said as she focused on Tim. "We've got another one."

"Another…?" Tim asked.

"Another fire, *and* another body," Ashley answered. "Sarah said she was…" she started to add before both her and Tim's phones alerted them to a notification. "Details for where we need to go."

Tim opened his phone up and took a few minutes to read through the details that had been provided.

Once he'd finished, he looked up at Ashley.

"Yet another town?" he asked out loud, more out of curiosity than needing the question answered. When he saw Ashley nod, Tim's mind started wandering. "Do you think there's any chance this is just an area arsonist at work?"

"And doesn't know there are people inside when they set up these places to explode?" Ashley asked and saw Tim nod. "But if that was the case, wouldn't they go out of their way to make sure that the people who live in the house definitely *wouldn't* be coming home?"

"True, but then if the people don't come home, the fires don't happen, with the way that the first two have been set up. If it's the explosion that they like, having people suffer from one happening might just be a necessary thing that they accept," said Tim. "Hmm, I'm definitely curious and keen to get to the bottom of this. Are you ready to go now?"

Ashley smiled sadly at him and nodded. She could sense his energy level having just shifted and increased. She knew that feeling well.

"Sarah did say that the same fire crew has attended this fire," said Ashley. "Let's go and talk to John Rogers at the station first. If it's already been six hours since the fire was reported and they went there, he must have some news by now, and perhaps a suspicion about whether this latest fire was set up by the same person or people who've done the last ones."

Tim nodded but said nothing more as he and Ashley made their way to the car and resumed their journey to the North Road Fire Station yet again.

CHAPTER 23

"I thought I'd be seeing you two again today," Captain John Rogers called out when he saw Ashley and Tim approach his office. "Come in and take a seat."

"Thank you," Ashley and Tim said before relaxing into the chairs they'd been directed to.

"Have you received some details that we should be aware of?" Tim asked, diving straight in without bothering with formalities or pleasantries.

In response to his question, he saw the captain look at him for a long while, not showing any emotion whatsoever as he did.

"I'm sure *you've* been sent details of this latest fire," John finally replied. "I'm guessing that's why you're here?"

Ashley studied his face before replying. It was easy to sense something not pleasant about the man in front of them. Strictly, Ashley pushed aside the uncertainty she naturally felt about him. She had a case to solve.

"Yes, we have received some details from the Bureau," she said. "I'm sure there will be more that will have come in since then, however. Is the circumstance the same as the fires at the Masters and Summers homes?"

"Yes," John said as he leaned forward and rubbed his eyes with his fingers. "This third one is remarkably similar. The investigation is just beginning, however there are already indications that it is the same. Same type of cut through the gas line."

"And same ... with a body inside?" Tim surmised and saw the captain nod in reply. "Just one?"

"One is more than enough, don't you think?" John quipped back, not looking in any way happy.

"Of course," Ashley said, curious about the dynamics happening before her eyes, but not wanting to focus on them. "You didn't know this victim?" she asked as a way to defuse whatever appeared to be brewing between her partner and the man she faced.

"No," John replied as he looked at her. "I have no contacts in that town, even though it's not too far from here." He paused for a long while as he opened a notebook that sat on the desk in front of him. "Mathew Spring is the owner and resident, so at this point, we're assuming it's him that's been found, but I'm guessing your side of the investigation will prove that to be the case - or not. But, no, the name isn't even familiar to me."

Tim glanced at Ashley and saw her do the same back at him. If there was any more new information to be gained from the North Road Fire Station, Captain John Rogers didn't look like he had anything to offer.

"I'm sorry I can't be of any more help," John said, looking from one agent to the other. "Just like the last two, the investigation will be carried out and then a report will be written."

Tim and Ashley remained quiet as they watched him reach into one of the drawers in his desk, and pulled out a large file.

"Here's the report from the Summers investigation, but for this third fire, I've instructed the scene investigators to email you directly," he said. "While I do need to have a copy of the reports, it's you guys who urgently need whatever's in them."

"Thank you," Ashley said as she grabbed the file being presented to her. "We'll head over to the scene now then, if there's nothing else you can tell us about this latest..."

"No," John replied. "Whatever there is to learn about this, you'll get more important details from the guys who should be on site by now."

"Thanks," Tim said before he and Ashley left the office.

Once out in the car, Ashley turned to face Tim, catching him just as he was about to say something.

"Yeah, I know," she said as she started the engine. "There's something off about him."

Tim grinned. He loved having a partner who knew him so well.

CHAPTER 24

"Another client of Date Today?" Tim asked when he and Ashley began to work through the details they'd received about the third victim. They'd already visited the scene of the latest fire, and spoken to the lead scene investigator. The similarities between the fires had the investigator worried, but their findings would be accessible via the report that would come in the following day.

"Looks like it," Ashley said, nodding. "All three of these guys were in that same dating site."

"Coincidence?" Tim asked. "There are a lot of dating sites out there these days. What's the chances that three guys who are on the same one, all die within such a short time of each other, and in the same way?"

"True," Ashley agreed. "Let's dig into the company behind it. You might be right about what you said earlier - maybe there's someone there who's read some of the goings on between members, and isn't too happy about it. Or maybe the company who runs it can tell us if there's been any particularly vicious threats towards them."

"You sound like you expect an actual human being to be at the end of a phone call, Ash," Tim said, chuckling. "I'm not sure that will turn out to be the case, but I'll put this through and get the tech guys to look into it. If there's a human to be chatted to, Tech'll probably be better at establishing a good rapport with them."

"I hope you aren't implying *again* that I'm not tech savvy, Special Agent Timothy Moore!" Ashley teased him.

Tim grinned at her but refrained from any witty comeback he might have felt trying to burst free.

"For now, let's just go through this new information we've received, Partner," he said diplomatically, glad to see the intended result of Ashley smiling before she then appeared to relax and refocus on the notes before them.

"Wait," Ashley said after a long while. "I thought this guy's name was Spring - Mathew Spring."

"Yep," Tim said.

"Then why am I looking at a document that's centered around a guy named Jeremy Olds?" asked Ashley. "Oh, wait. That was his alias? Jeremy Olds?"

"Seems like it. Plus Jeremy Young, and Jeremy Wright, according to this," Tim said as he pointed out the victim's various names that had been identified. "I think I can see why, too. Look at this," he continued. "The age ranges of women he was in contact with."

"You have got to be kidding," Ashley said in surprise. "He was chatting up elderly women, using the surname, 'Olds', and young women under the surname, 'Young'?"

"Yep, looks like it," said Tim. "And this one - 'Wright' - looks like what he used for chatting up women around his actual age."

"And all of these are actually Mathew Spring?" Ashley asked. "This isn't some typo from somewhere along the line of documentation?"

"No, with these notes and links, it's correct that Mathew Spring *is* Jeremy Olds, Jeremy Young, and Jeremy Wright," Tim confirmed.

"And if he's targeting women of such specific age groups, using completely fake names, can we guess that he's going to turn out to be a catfish as well?" Ashley asked.

"Yeah, it definitely looks like it, Ash," said Tim. "That gives us three things that these guys all have in common - they're all in dating websites, they're all in Date Today, and it does seem like they've all been trying to somehow gain financially from the women they interact with."

"Okay," Ashley said as she began pondering all that they knew. "So our first victim - Bob Masters - was repeatedly trying to get cash out of people… well, deposits into his bank account at least."

"Right - one thousand dollars was his go-to amount to ask for," Tim agreed. "And he did that entirely without ever meeting or facing any of the women in person."

"Our second victim, Lance Summers, was luring women to lush hotels and doing some sneaky big-order thing while they thought he was just being nice and suggesting they treat themselves to a long luxury bath," Ashley added.

"Correct," said Tim. "Seduced them and made them feel like queens for a day, while surprisingly successfully getting loads of stuff charged to the room, and their credit cards."

"Then … what has Jeremy - Mathew - been trying to get out of anyone?" Ashley asked as she began shuffling through documents open on her laptop screen.

"Looking at these conversations, it's hard to know," said Tim. "He's been a lot more discreet than the last two, as far as digital words go. One thing that's interesting with this guy's conversations, though, is that he's mentioned going to see some of his victims. These older ones, especially - the ones who thought they were talking to Jeremy Olds."

"Oh," Ashley said as her laptop made the ping sound that said a new email had arrived. After she'd opened it and read it, she turned to Tim. "Looks like we now know why he didn't use his real name. Mathew Spring was investigated a couple of years ago."

"For what?" asked Tim.

"Someone alerted police to this guy having used his charm to work over an elderly woman, and establish himself as someone she should leave her entire estate to," said Ashley.

"Wow, okay. And did that happen? Did he successfully get her estate after she died?" Tim asked.

"Yeah, looks like it," Ashley replied as she read more. "Her daughter was left with nothing."

"Sounds like that might be a perfect reason to get rid of him," said Tim. "When did this happen? Two years ago, did you say?"

"Hmm … no, yes. Wait. Oh, he met the woman *five* years ago, and the investigation was completed *two* years ago," Ashley said. "That's quite a long background, but he could definitely still have been doing this kind of thing."

"Yeah, especially if he'd been investigated before and knew he could get away with it," said Tim.

"We might need to chase up this woman's family and have a chat," Ashley suggested.

"And the families of the other elderly women he's been chatting to as well," Tim said. "If he *did* think he'd proven it was easy to get away with something like that, it's entirely possible - probable, even - that he's continued to do it."

"That would make perfect sense about why he's using multiple aliases," Ashley agreed. "Must be hard for people like this to stay online once one person's already become suspicious about them."

"We can only hope," said Tim. "Unfortunately, the reverse is true most of the time. After the first time of ripping someone off, even if they just fluked it, they not only get what they want, but they learn from the experience too. With each new target they find, they're just that little bit better at doing what they want to do, getting what they want, and then getting away with it."

"Well, this guy is now dead," said Ashley. "If he thought he was never going to pay for whatever it is that he was doing, he just might have been proven wrong. Mr Spring…"

"Was finally sprung," Tim said, finishing her sentence.

Ashley grinned at his attempt at humor before refocusing on all that she had to read through. They'd received a lot of information, but once they'd worked through it all, there was no doubt that the latest victim of a gas explosion and fire had also been trying hard to get as much as he could out of members of the opposite gender.

"Again, this guy appears to have only targeted women," Ashley said after a long while. "We have seen men get targeted by catfish as well, but this lot - well, they all seem to be focused only on women."

"Yeah, it does surprise me that they don't appear to have broadened their catfish horizons," said Tim. "I'm sure there are just as many lonely men out there as there are women."

"It does seem to be an intense level of loneliness that drives people to want to be generous towards others," Ashley agreed. "It's just so sad when the generosity of a good person is so blatantly twisted and used for someone else's own agenda."

"I know, but if everyone was nice, Ash, we probably wouldn't have a job," Tim said, smiling sadly at her.

"So true, oh wise one!" Ashley replied. "Okay, well, let's see if we can find the daughter of the person we know, for certain, Mathew took for a ride."

"Yep, and by then, the tech guys will have established a full list of all of his online victims, hopefully," said Tim. "Once we have that, we'll be able to see what else he's been trying to get out of people."

"Of course, there's always the chance that he hasn't been trying to get *anything* out of the people he's established rapport with online," Ashley said. "He might not end up being exactly like the previous two victims after all."

"There is always a chance of that," Tim agreed. "But I'm putting my money on it being more likely that Mathew Spring has at least *tried* to rip someone off. If he hasn't, then we have other avenues to look down to try and find out who might have wanted to hurt him."

Both agents remained silent for a long while as they each pondered any other possible relationship there could be between the men who had been killed. The silent thoughts of Ashley and Tim were interrupted by the sound of Tim's phone.

"We've got the last known address of the daughter of the elderly client he ripped off. She's about thirty minutes from here," Tim said. "We've also got addresses for a couple of other elderly women that this guy was in contact with right before he was killed. Looks like one is at a residential address. The other address looks like the name of a rest home."

"Great," said Ashley as she shut down her laptop and grabbed her things. "Let's hit the road and see if we can piece together just why, as you put it, Mr Spring was sprung!"

CHAPTER 25

"Can I help you?" the middle aged man asked when he'd opened the front door of his home to Ashley and Tim.

"Hello, I'm Special Agent Power and this is Special Agent Moore," Ashley said. "We're trying to find a Miss Gabana…"

"Meg Gabana?" the man asked.

"Yes," Ashley replied. "Do you know where we can find her?"

"Meg!" the man called out inside the house before opening the door wide and silently inviting Ashley and Tim to enter. "Not Gabana now," he added. "Meg's my wife. She now goes by the surname of Tarlton."

"Yeah?" Ashley heard a woman call out before she reached the foyer where Tim and Ashley stood. "Oh. Can I help you?"

"We hope so," Ashley said. "We understand you know something of a man named Mathew Spring…"

As Ashley spoke, she and Tim both noticed the expression on the woman's face.

"Who's he ripped off now?" Meg asked.

"You do know who we mean?" Tim asked, just to be sure.

"Of course I do," Meg said as she guided the agents to sit down in the living room. "Asshole did a real number on my mother. To this day, I … ugh … it makes my blood boil just thinking about him and what he did."

"Can you tell us about your interactions with Mr Spring, Meg?" Ashley asked.

"Interactions?" Meg asked with a scoff and an incredulous look on her face. "I had no interactions with that coward. He wouldn't face me - not when he was working my mother over, and definitely not since my mother died and he got everything she'd ever worked hard to own." She paused, appearing to try to remain calm. "Has he done it again? Is that why you've tracked me down?"

"We don't know," said Ashley. "It is an ongoing investigation, but we can tell you that Mr Spring is dead."

Tim watched the face of the woman in front of them. While he didn't expect her to be sad that the victim was no longer among the living, he was surprised by how little emotion of any kind there was on her face. After a long period of silence, he saw her finally speak.

"I know I'll sound callous when I say this, but I can't say I'm saddened by that news ... or surprised, come to think of it," Meg said. "He wasn't a good person."

"He hurt your mother?" Ashley asked, not sure how things had panned out once everything of Mrs Gabana's had been transferred to Mr Spring.

"No," Meg replied, shaking her head in obvious dismay. "For the last months of her life, she was happy. She'd been conned - we all could see that - but I can't deny that in her inability to see what was happening, she thought she'd found some kind of new ... *soul mate* before she died. Nobody could believe it, but it was what it was. If that asshole's dead ... well, there's nothing to fight for now, is there. Everything that he'd gotten out of her will be well and truly gone,

I'm guessing."

"Had you hoped to recoup something of your mother's?" Ashley asked.

"No, not really," Meg said with a sad smile on her face. "It was wishful dreaming, I guess. I didn't care about her money so much, but there were family heirlooms - things that had been in my mother's family for several generations. They were the things that I was most upset about. I have kids. All of that stuff could have been passed to another generation." She paused for a long while before speaking again. "What … shit … sorry … how exactly do you think I might be able to help you with whatever you're looking into?"

"We mostly wanted to know if you've seen or heard from him in recent times," said Tim.

"No. Like I say, he never interacted with me at all," Meg replied. "Honestly, even when I went to visit Mom at the rest home, sometimes it would seem like he'd literally *just* left there - almost like he'd been watching the carpark and seen me arriving, and slipped out the back door as I was entering. Sorry but there's really nothing that I can tell you, other than he charmed my mother, and he was successful in getting her to change her will. I don't know how he did it, but he was incredibly successful at making her believe there must have been a real reason why she'd be better off leaving everything to him rather than her own family."

"Were there problems between you and your mother at that time?" Tim asked, curious.

"I wish I could say there was a reason like that for her to have changed her will, but no," said Meg. "My mom and I were always close - well, I might have been a little rebellious in my teenage years," she added, with a chuckle. "But, no, when I got married and began giving her grandkids, everything was wonderful, and she seemed just the same before she died. I mean, she looked like a woman who'd met the man of her dreams ... but she was always the same towards me."

"Do you think your mother was swayed by him to think less of you, or..."

"Surprisingly, no," Meg replied. "As far as I know, I don't think he purposely talked her into leaving nothing to me. He just talked her into leaving *everything* to him."

"Was he murdered?" Meg's husband asked, bringing immediate attention to himself.

Tim studied the face of the man before answering.

"Mr Spring's death is still being investigated," he replied. "Can I ask..." he began, redirecting a new question to Meg. "Your mother didn't know Mr Spring by that name, did she?"

"No," Meg replied. "When she was talking about him, she always called him Jeremy. Jeremy this, and Jeremy that. She'd prattle on about how wonderful he was."

"Right. May I ask how have you made the connection about his name?" Ashley asked, curious.

"Oh, it was after the will was read," Meg said. "I don't know how it came about, but when the will was read, they kept talking about how everything had been left to Mathew Spring. I had no idea who that was. It was the lawyer who explained to me that he'd received instruction from my mother, to change her will and to address both names in it - Jeremy Olds and Mathew Spring. There was some legal jargon that the lawyer talked about, but I tuned out to it. I was in enough surprise when he explained to me in more simple terms that the man who my mother had left everything to - Jeremy Olds - was in fact actually called Mathew

Spring. I asked him if that was legal - that a will can state one person with two names to inherit everything. He said that some clause or other in the document made it all perfectly legit. For a while, I looked into instigating contesting the will, but it was always in the back of my mind that even though it made no sense to me, and certainly didn't make me happy, it *was* what my mother had wanted. In the end, I decided not to fight it. She had her reasons for doing things how she had. It wasn't my place to question her actions."

"Forgive me for asking, but was your mother of sound mind when she changed her will?" Tim asked.

"Oh, yes," Meg replied. "I do understand your question, and I was wondering the same thing, but the people who were around her reassured me that she was certainly of sound mind before she passed. If she hadn't been, I probably would have gone ahead and contested the will, based on that, but I had to put faith in what the health professionals were telling me. At the end of the day, she knew what she was doing, and she wanted to do it, so all I could do was respect her choice. Like I said, the cash and the big stuff wasn't important to me, but family heirlooms - they were the most upsetting things to lose, especially to someone like that."

"I see," Ashley said, intrigued. Glancing at Tim, she could see that he'd reached the same conclusion that she had - that there was little more for them to learn from the woman they were speaking to. "Well, thank you for your help..."

"Is there any chance you could find out what happens with Mom's family things now?" Meg asked as they all stood and began to walk toward the front door.

Ashley stopped and looked at the woman, feeling surprisingly sad for her.

"Mr Spring died in a fire in his home, so not much has survived that, but we can certainly ask for you," she said. "Are you able to make a list of things you mean, or maybe find some photos for us? Here's my card, with an email address you're welcome to contact me on with any details. We can't promise anything, but we're happy to at least ask the fire scene investigators if anything that was your mother's seems to have been at the scene, and survived. Other than that, you could talk to your lawyer. Perhaps Mr Spring stored the things that he got from your mother's estate somewhere else - in a storage unit or something - but speak to your lawyer. I'm sure they can best advise you."

"Yes, I will do that. Thank you," said Meg as she watched Tim and Ashley walk out the door. "I know it's a long shot, but no harm in asking, right?"

Tim and Ashley smiled and then turned to walk down the long path to the car. Once seated inside, and Ash had started the engine, Tim turned to face her.

"Thoughts?" he asked.

"I feel bad for her," Ashley admitted. "But however bad that situation is for her - and for her late mother - there's not a lot that can be done about it now."

"You gave her a bit of hope…"

"I know," said Ashley. "Even if some of those things are in the house, I suspect she'd have to go through some legal nightmare to get them back into her ownership, especially if it was all legally transferred by will, but we are in contact with the scene investigators so, as she said, no harm in asking if anything of her mother's might have at least survived the fire."

"The husband was interesting," Tim said, thoughtful. "Overall, he didn't have too much to say, even though it must have been a horrific episode in his wife's life."

"Yeah, him asking if Spring had been murdered did surprise me," Ashley agreed. "Meg hadn't even asked how he'd died."

"Maybe because she already knew..." Tim pondered.

"Let's look into the background of both of them," Ashley suggested. "For now, we need to go speak to these more recent targets of Spring's."

CHAPTER 26

"We're here to talk to a Mrs Sarah Sharp," Tim said when he and Ashley approached the receptionist at Bonnie Days Rest Home. Holding up his ID, he gave the woman behind the desk a smile. "Special Agents Tim Moore and Ashley Power from the Bureau of Investigation."

"It isn't possible for me to let you in to see any of our residents straight away, but I'll let the manager know that you're here," the receptionist said with no friendliness in her voice.

Ashley glanced at Tim as they both heard the woman behind the protective window talk on the phone.

"She'll be right out," she said when she'd finished her call.

"Can I help you?" Ashley and Tim heard another woman call out to them. Turning, both saw her walking swiftly toward them.

"Yes, we would like to talk to one of your residents - Mrs Sarah Sharp," Tim said.

"Of course. We should be able to arrange that, but first please come through to my office," the woman said, turning sharply and walking away again.

As Ashley glanced at Tim, she saw a very subtle rolling of the eyes. They hadn't expected any problem at all in their desire to talk to a rest home resident. Both could see it wasn't as easy to do such a thing as they'd hoped.

Inside the small office they were shown to, nobody spoke until all were seated.

"Thank you for your patience, but we do have a policy here about visits to our residents," the woman said. "Cybil Douglas", she added as she held out her hand, finally introducing herself.

"I'm Special Agent Ashley Power, and this is Special Agent Tim Moore," Ashley said. "As we said, we would very much like to talk to Sarah Sharp."

"Yes," Cybil said as she relaxed back in her chair and regarded both agents. "What is this about? I can't see how any of my residents could be in trouble…"

"Oh, no," Tim quickly said. "No, we are hoping to talk to her, to actually see if she can help us with an investigation."

"Investigation?" Cybil asked and was greeted by Ashley and Tim both nodding in reply. "Into what?"

"Into a gentleman who's been found dead," Ashley replied. "We understand there might be a chance that Mrs Sharp had some kind of … romantic … interest in this person."

"This man's name isn't Jeremy by any chance, is it?" Cybil asked. When Tim confirmed that to be the case, she instantly picked up her phone. "Please locate Alice and ask her to come to my office immediately," she said before hanging up the phone and looking at the agents again. "Alice is a nurse here. Being a day nurse, she has the closest relationship with Sarah. A while back, she brought some concerns to me. I think she might be able to answer any questions you have about this."

Before Tim or Ashley could ask the manager any further questions, a knock was heard on the door.

"Yes!" Cybil called out, prompting a member of staff to enter.

"You wanted to see me?" the nurse asked as she

glanced from agent to agent and then to her boss.

"Yes, come in and grab a seat, Alice," Cybil said. "These agents…"

"Ashley Power, and this is Tim Moore," Ashley said as she interpreted the question in Cybil's voice and glance.

"They are here to talk to Sarah Sharp," Cybil finished.

"Oh?" Alice asked, curious. "Has something happened?"

"You are aware of Mrs Sharp having some contact with a man named…" Ashley began to ask before her question was cut short.

"Jeremy?" Alice asked and saw Ashley nod in reply. "Oh, yes. Sarah … well, let's just say that Sarah was enraptured with him."

"Was?" Tim asked, picking up on the past tense of the words that had been used. "She isn't any longer?"

Ashley saw the nurse look at her and Tim for a long time before she answered the question.

"With regard to Sarah's … *relationship* … with him, there were some … *concerns*," Alice said.

"What kind of concerns do you mean?" Ashley asked, and immediately saw the nurse move uncomfortably in her seat.

"Mrs Sharp … let me firstly say that she is an absolutely lovely lady," Alice said. "She lost her husband almost twenty years ago, and her kids put her in here not long after, claiming she wasn't able to live alone."

"You sound unsure…" Tim said, curious about the way the nurse was talking.

"It's just that … well … I've been here the entire time that Sarah has," Alice continued. "From the first day she was here, I've always thought she was a lovely, independent and strong woman. There was nothing about her that indicated to me that she *couldn't* live alone, but her being in here was what her kids wanted, so she didn't argue with them."

"And over the time that she's been here?" Ashley asked. "Has she continued to be that same person?"

"In most ways, yes," said Alice. "But of course, over time, she has had times when she's implied that she's been lonely. Most people I see in here do have times like that, even though it is a social environment and the residents do seem to have fun here."

"And the residents have access to the outside world via the Internet?" Tim asked, looking from the nurse to the rest home manager.

"Oh, yes, of course!" Alice replied. "Yes, and I do think that is how Sarah happened to meet Jeremy. A few of the other residents had been talking for a while about using the computer to make contact with new people. I don't think Sarah used it straight away, but yes, I believe she eventually decided to give it a go, and then somehow stumbled upon him that way."

"Can you tell us more about what happened between them?" asked Tim. "I get the impression from what you're saying that something wasn't quite right. Did they actually meet? In person?"

"Oh, yes," said Alice. "He came here quite a few times. After each visit, Sarah was ... *alight*, I guess is a good word to describe it. Honestly, after each time she saw that man, she looked like she was a new bride. Absolutely *beaming*, she was."

"How did the staff and the other residents feel about the two of them spending time together?" Ashley asked. "Did anyone see anything bad in it? There must have been quite an age gap..."

"Yes, when she was looking forward to meeting him, I thought she'd implied he wasn't much younger than her," Alice said. "When he'd visited that first time, I asked her who the man was that I'd seen leaving her room. Because of his age, I assumed it must have been someone from her family - someone she hadn't mentioned, like a nephew, or maybe even a *grandson*. But it wasn't. When she told me it was 'her Jeremy', I didn't ask her about it, but I did feel confused. I was so sure it would have been a man much older that she'd been referring to when she'd talked about him. She'd certainly never said she was chatting to a guy *that* much younger!"

"Please continue," Tim encouraged her when he watched her expression change to one of almost disbelief.

"Yes, well, he came a few times, and after each visit, whenever I'd see Sarah, she'd rave about him, but over time, with each subsequent visit he made, she started to look sadder and sadder," Alice said. "When I asked her why, she said something had happened to him, and he knew he was in trouble financially so wouldn't be able to come and see her very often anymore. Sarah sounded awfully sad about it, so I felt a bit sorry for her. I had no reason to think she wasn't telling the truth to me - I mean, why would she lie about that? She didn't have to tell me anything at all, so why would she talk to me about something, but not be truthful? I had no reason to disbelieve her, and so I didn't think anything about any of it."

"Then what happened?" asked Ashley.

"Then, one day when I was in town, I saw him," said Alice. "At first, I thought it couldn't be him, but when I looked and looked, I was sure. It *was* him. Well, I didn't know what to think because Sarah had been saying that he was poor - almost to the point of being destitute, with the way that she described it. But there he was, dressed to the nines, in a sports car, with a young woman who looked like a glamour model beside him! There was nothing about the scene that made me think he was poor - quite the opposite!"

"What was your thought then?" Tim asked and saw her glance at him with a hardened look on her face.

"I thought then that he wasn't real, and he hadn't been truthful with Sarah at all," Alice replied. "At first, I said nothing about it. I didn't want to upset Sarah, and for all I knew, maybe it was over with anyway. If he was disappearing from her life because he'd found someone younger, he was going to break her heart anyway. I wasn't prepared to hurt her more by telling her he'd been lying to her about his state of living."

"So you did nothing?" Ashley asked.

"I wasn't sure what to do at first, but then I knew I couldn't bring myself to say anything to Sarah," Alice said. "It did keep playing on my mind, though. Whenever she'd talk to me, I felt bad because I wasn't being fully open and honest with her. In the end, I talked to a few other members of staff, including Mrs Douglas here. Everyone thought it best to not say anything to Sarah. We were all sure that the guy would disappear, and when he did, it would be easier for Sarah if she didn't know just how much he'd deceived her."

"And did he do that? Just disappear?" Tim asked.

"No," said Alice. "One day he strolled in here, just like every other time he had, and went to talk to her. I was worried, but said nothing and just went about my day. The next day, Sarah told me that she wanted to change her will to make sure he'd be okay and well looked after. I was … well, I was *mortified*."

"You mean she wanted to change it … to include him?" asked Tim.

"No, not just include him, but replace all of her kids and grandkids with him as the full recipient of her entire estate!" Alice replied. "I ... I couldn't understand why she would even think to do it. I knew her kids had put her in here, maybe even before she *needed* to come here, but all of her kids have been in at some stage or other to see her. I mean, sure, they don't seem to be a close knit family, exactly, but there doesn't seem to be any reason on either side for her to exclude them from her will completely. I never saw them argue or be disrespectful. They weren't close, but, from what I've seen and heard, there equally didn't appear to be any disharmony or disagreement between them. No, with regards to her taking the whole lot of them out of her will and giving it all to a young man who she thought was poor but certainly didn't look like it, it just wasn't right!"

"What did you do when you found out about her intentions?" Tim asked.

"I talked to the other staff again, and explained what I'd learned," said Alice. "Everyone was worried about it. I know it's not our concern, what our residents do with any of their assets, but we were all concerned that she was making a mistake. Mrs Douglas here said there's nothing legally that we can do about such things, so nothing could be reported or anything, but I felt..." she said as she placed a hand on her stomach. "I felt *sick* at the idea that Sarah might have been fooled by someone, and she and her family could be the ones to suffer from it all. She's such a lovely woman."

"So nothing was ever done about it?" asked Tim.

"Nothing *could* be done," Cybil said. "Not by us anyway."

"And did she change her will, do you know?" Tim asked.

"A lawyer came and visited her a few days later," Alice confirmed. "Sarah didn't say anything about what had happened, and I didn't ask. At the end of the day, our residents are still their own people, and who are we to judge what someone's intentions are. I know that Jeremy didn't hurt her physically in any way. If he managed to successfully get something financial out of her, I really don't know."

Tim looked at Ashley and then glanced at each of the two members of staff.

"Is it possible for us to talk to Mrs Sharp?" he asked the rest home manager. "Does she know?"

"About what?" Alice asked.

"The man you and Sarah met - Jeremy - has been found dead," Ashley answered.

"We've only found out about it with you coming here and telling us, Agents," Cybil said.

"Yes, but is there any chance she has mentioned his death to you already?" Ashley asked the nurse.

"No, she hasn't said anything to me," Alice replied. "If it has just happened, how would…" she began to ask before seeming to realize that might be exactly why the agents were there. "Sarah … no, you cannot think that Sarah could contribute to someone's death?! Did he kill himself? Do you think he did that because of her? I'm so confused. What is it, exactly, that you need to know?"

Watching the nurse grow agitated, Tim was perplexed. In all the minutes they'd been in the same room before that moment, Alice Brown had seemed calm and caring. On hearing the question about whether Sarah already knew Jeremy was dead, Alice's demeanor had changed immensely.

"We would like to talk to her, if that is possible," Ashley said to Cybil. "May we please?"

"Yes, of course," the manager replied. "Alice, please show Sarah and the agents to the private lounge, so they may speak in private."

After a long moment of looking uncertain, Alice appeared to gather herself before she stood and silently guided Ashley and Tim out of the office.

"You seem tentative about us speaking to Sarah," Tim said as they walked down a small corridor.

"Yes, sorry," Alice replied. "I've known Sarah for so long, and to be honest, this whole thing has made me nervous. I wish I hadn't seen Jeremy that day in town, with his sports car, and rich clothing, and a young, pretty woman at his side. I've wanted to tell Sarah, but I know that could cause her pain. Still, all we ever want for the people that we care about is for them to never hurt."

"Yes, of course," Ashley said as they were shown into a small room.

"Please take a seat and I'll bring Sarah to you shortly," the nurse added before walking off.

"Interesting conversation," Tim muttered to Ashley when they were alone. "Places like this have always made me nervous."

"Oh?" Ashley asked, curious. In her years of working cases with Tim, she'd grown to believe it was rare for *anything* to make him nervous. "Do you think you won't get old and eventually live somewhere like this?" she went on to tease him.

"Don't even say such a thing, Special Agent Ashley Power!" Tim replied, grinning at her. "I'm never going to get old, and neither are you!"

Ashley chuckled. He still managed to surprise her sometimes. She liked that.

CHAPTER 27

"Hello, Mrs Sharp," Tim greeted the elderly woman as he watched her enter the small room with Alice by her side. "I'm Tim Moore, and this is Ashley Power. We'd like to talk to you, if we can."

Ashley watched the elderly woman smile before accepting Tim's handshake.

"How can I help you?" Sarah asked.

"If you're happy to talk to these agents, Sarah, come and get settled over here," Alice said as she gently began to guide the elderly woman. "You'll be nice and comfortable here."

No more words were said until Ashley, Tim, and the rest home resident were seated in their armchairs and the door was closed.

"We'd like to talk to you about a man named Jeremy, Mrs Sharp," Ashley began. As soon as she mentioned his name, she could see a mix of confused emotions flow over the elderly woman's face. "You do know who we mean?"

"Yes, of course," Sarah replied. "He … he is … I am not sure what to say now. I don't know how to talk about him."

"Why is that?" Tim asked. He wondered how alert the elderly woman in front of him might be, given how old she was. When she began to talk, he could see that his perception of old age wasn't accurate. The woman before him was eloquent, and definitely aware of what was happening around her.

"Jeremy seemed so nice at first," Sarah said. "When you get to my age … well, let me just say that he was a breath of fresh air - especially in this place, with all the old fuddy duddies!" she added, making Tim and Ashley smile.

"We understand that you were considering changing your will after you met him a few times," Ashley said. "Sorry to have to ask, Mrs Sharp, but did you do that?"

Tim watched the face of the elderly woman relax before she smiled at him and Ashley again.

"I almost did," she finally answered. "I felt sorry for him. He seemed lonely, and down on his luck. After a few of the staff and other residents here said that I should be more careful and take longer to think about it, I realized that I shouldn't rush into such a thing." She paused for a long while before speaking again. "The staff here are so wonderful, you know. When that happened, they showed me just how much they do care about me," she added as her eyes began to water.

"Alice, do you mean?" Ashley asked.

"Alice, yes," Sarah said as she nodded. "Alice, and John - another nurse - and even that nice young man, Dean, who's an orderly here. They're all chatty, but when that happened, they all showed just how much they *care*."

"You did see your lawyer about the will though?" Tim asked.

"I did," Alice confirmed. "I made the appointment, with the intention of changing my will. When I talked to him, that was the final encouragement I needed to convince me that I shouldn't."

"Your *lawyer* told you that you shouldn't change your will?" Ashley asked.

"No," said Alice. "Oh no, well not exactly. He also

told me to take more time to think about it."

"I see," said Ashley, her mind pondering a new possibility.

"But what has brought you here today, may I ask?" Sarah asked. "Is Jeremy in trouble?"

"No," Ashley said. "Unfortunately, Mrs Sharp, we are sorry to say that Mr … Jeremy … has died."

As Ashley broke the news, Tim watched the elderly woman's face closely. It was sometimes revealing, seeing someone's facial expression when they learned something new - or were told something that wasn't new to them at all.

"Oh, heavens!" Sarah exclaimed. "How awful! How did it happen?"

"We are still investigating the details of his death," Ashley said quietly. "Is there anything about him that you can remember that might help in our investigation?"

"I'm not sure what you mean," Sarah said, her tone taking on a harder sound.

"How did you meet Jeremy?" Tim asked.

"We began chatting on one of those … dating places, on the computer … dating sites, I think they're called," Sarah said. "Date … Today? I think that's what it was called, but my memory isn't what it used to be."

"And did he approach you first in the site, or you approached him?"

"He approached me," Sarah replied, with a small smile on her face. "Quite charming, he was too. Of course, I did think he was a little older … but he said that those sites often mix up the people they match."

"You didn't mind when you met and saw he was younger than you thought?" Tim asked.

"No," Sarah said, laughing softly. "I didn't expect I'd see him again after that. If he looked younger to me, I suspected I must have looked downright ancient to him! But he still talked to me, and still came to see me."

"Did you develop feelings for one another?" asked Ashley.

"I think … I think that I was charmed by him," said Sarah. "Feelings? I'm not sure if that is an accurate description. It did feel positive at the time, but what is ever real? By the time you reach my age, you will see that most things you see and are told, you hope are true, but know they very rarely are."

"How do you feel about him now?" Ashley asked.

"I feel sad that you've told me he's passed away," Sarah said, her tone once again changing. "But for a while … for a little while … he was a joy to be around. When you find a little joy in your life, be sure to embrace it. Don't be afraid of it when it happens, and don't be afraid of it ending. Everything that begins must end. What's important is that you see it for the joy that it is for that time. Remember that."

"Thank you, Sarah," said Tim, smiling at her. "Sometimes I do think we all need to be reminded of exactly that."

"Yes, it is a harsh reality of life," Sarah said. "I am sorry I cannot think of any way that I could help you with whatever it is that you wish to find out."

"You have helped us, Sarah," said Ashley. It was the truth. They'd wondered if the charm of 'Jeremy' was still enough to rip older women off. It was a refreshing discovery to learn that with at least one woman, it hadn't quite been enough after all.

Sensing Sarah's indication that she had nothing more to say, Tim and Ashley thanked her, said goodbye, and left the room.

"Was she able to be of assistance?" they heard Alice call out as they exited the lounge door.

"Yes, thank you!" Ashley called back.

Walking through the rest home, toward the exit, she looked around. Spread through various rooms were residents taking part in one activity or another. Scattered among them were a number of members of staff, all smiling and seeming to do their jobs with respect and a sense of ease and fun.

"Staff board," Ashley heard Tim say. When she looked at him, she saw him pointing at a wall of photos.

"Anyone of interest up there?" Ashley asked.

"At this stage, it's hard to know who exactly is - or will be - a person of interest," Tim replied as he took time to glance at each face before him.

Ashley focused on the faces for a long while before turning to focus on Tim again.

"There isn't much more we can do here for the moment," she said. "Lunch?"

Tim grinned at her and glanced at the staff photos one more time before nodding and turning.

"Perfect idea, Special Agent Ashley Power."

CHAPTER 28

Determined to find a more solid connection between all three victims, and the ways they died, Ashley and Tim returned to North Road Fire Department later that afternoon.

"The report is in regarding Mathew Spring," said Tim as they entered the large building. "Hopefully something will be in it that'll provide us with a clue."

"Something definitely has to happen soon, to help us solve this case," Ashley said. "Preferably before someone else gets hurt."

"Well, we know all three were on dating sites, and all could have been on Date Today, but there has to be a closer link between these victims," Tim said. "You know I'm not big on the idea of coincidences at the best of times, but I can't imagine the odds are high that there's no further common ground between these guys. Nothing's impossible, but..."

"More common ground than just them being on Date Today, you mean?" asked Ashley.

"Yes!" Tim exclaimed. "They've all been doing a similar thing, and in a common place where they all found their online victims, but what's making them all worthy of what's happened to them? Why them and not the other thousands of people in the same dating site?"

"Let's see what this latest report tells us," Ashley said. It wasn't common for her partner to get so riled up, but she could see that he was.

"Yes, it's here," they heard John Rogers call out as they approached his office.

In his hands, Ashley could see the thick file he held. She didn't hesitate in her approach to accept it from him.

"There's nothing new in there, though," John said. "Honestly, if I didn't know these were three different events, I'd wonder if I'm reading the same report."

"Everything is the same?" Tim asked as he sat down.

"Well, not everything, obviously, but the reason behind the fire? Yep," said John. "Same thing - a clean cut right through the gas line."

"And that's what started the fire," Ashley mumbled as she glanced at the text on the paper she held.

"That's what ignited the small explosion, which then created the fire," John confirmed. "Just like the others."

Tim looked at Ashley. Although she had her sight centered on the pages on her lap, he could see her level of concentration. The report was something Tim knew they couldn't read in a hurry, but the way Ashley was skimming the pages, he was confident she'd see something stand out if there was anything of immediate urgency to see.

"Are you making leeway on this investigation?" he heard the station captain ask. "Seems like these explosions are continuing, even with you so close."

Tim shifted his gaze to the man. Several times, John had used the same tone when speaking to Ashley and Tim. It wasn't reason enough to make him highly suspicious, but it certainly got Tim's attention when the tone moved from friendly to bordering on aggressive.

"It's an ongoing..." Tim began to say.

"An ongoing investigation," John said, cutting the

sentence short. "Yeah, I know. But I hope you find out what's going on soon. These fires are killing people."

Although she'd been trying to focus on glancing over the report, the last sentence John had said prompted Ashley to look up. There wasn't any untruth in what he'd said - people *were* dying, and had been even since she and Tim had arrived in the area. There was still something unnerving about how it had been said.

"As soon as we know something, we'll be sure to let you know," Tim said, not sure what the man in front of them intended for them to be able to say. John wasn't in law enforcement, so surely didn't expect some kind of report about the state of the case...

"Well, I'm glad we've got all three scene investigation reports now," Ashley said as she forced a smile onto her face. "Can we take this copy?"

"Yes, of course," John said, his tone suddenly changing again to one of friendliness as he returned a smile toward Ashley.

"Thank you," Ashley said before turning to face Tim. "Shall we?"

"Sure," Tim replied. They weren't anywhere close to solving the case, but there seemed little more that they'd be able to learn from the fire department that had attended all three fires.

Without saying anything more, Ashley led the way out of the office.

"Hopefully we won't have to come back here," Tim said as they made their way down to the lower level of the station again. "Where to now..." he began to ask before noticing that Ashley had stopped walking and was looking at the wall of photos of the department's firefighters. "What is it?"

"What? Oh, nothing," Ashley said, looking at each of the photos. "I didn't really notice these before, that's all."

Tim focused on the portrait photos that Ashley had pointed to.

"Uhuh," Tim said in preparation to tease her. "I'm guessing you're one of those people who hangs out for a 'hot firemen' calendar every year then?"

"Haha," Ashley retorted. "I can honestly say that is one thing I've *never* bought, Timothy Moore!"

"Sure," Tim said, teasing her further.

"I'm guessing you'll be wanting to take some time now to dive in and read that report from start to end then?" Ashley asked as she turned away from the wall, determined to not let her partner tease her any more.

"Sure thing, Partner."

CHAPTER 29

As Tim worked his way through the fire scene investigation report, Ashley took some time to review all that she had on her laptop about everything to do with the case so far. As usual in the middle of an investigation, she'd started to feel like they weren't really getting anywhere. She trusted that would change - it always did eventually. It just took the right thread to begin to unravel.

"John Rogers wasn't wrong in what he told us," Tim said, looking up from the pages. "Even though each of these fires was different, with them being at different kinds of houses and burning in different ways, there really is a lot in here that is the same as the other reports."

"Yeah, when I glanced through it, I wasn't sure there would be anything in it that would help us in this investigation," Ashley agreed. "The essential point is that the reports do indicate that someone intentionally cut those gas lines..."

"Presumably with the intention of hurting someone," Tim added.

"Yeah, well, I guess that, with the first one, that might not have been the intention," Ashley said. "It could have been an arson attack, with no desire to hurt anyone."

"But if it's the same person who's gone on to do the second and third explosion, they did, by then, know that what they'd done - tampering with the gas line -

can result in someone's death," said Tim. "I'll grant you the possibility that the first death could have been an unforeseen error by an arsonist, but I can't consider that the second and third instances were. By then, I do think that whoever's doing this had full knowledge that their cutting of those lines might very possibly result in someone being killed."

"True," Ashley agreed. "What keeps popping into the forefront of my mind now is whether we're going to get to this person before they strike again. I can't stand the thought of another explosion and another bod…"

"We'll find them, Ash," Tim reassured her.

The sound of both of their phones alerting them to notifications stopped the negative thinking of both agents.

"Sarah Sharp…" Tim started to say when he read the message that had reached his phone.

"Let's go," Ashley added as she started to shut down the screen of her laptop, then secure it in the room safe.

"It doesn't say what happened," said Tim, feeling heaviness in his heart.

"No," Ashley agreed as they rushed out to the car. "We'll find out soon enough."

During the journey to Bonnie Days Rest Home, Tim and Ashley said nothing. As they pulled up the driveway to the home, they were greeted by the sight of an ambulance. With heavy hearts, both agents could tell it was in no hurry to get to wherever it would ultimately be going.

"Agents," they heard the rest home manager, Cybil Douglas, call out to them as they entered. "You've received the news, I take it."

"We weren't sure what happened," Ashley said.

"She was found a little while ago," Cybil said. "It

is a great loss."

"I'm so sorry to hear that, but thank you for letting us know," Ashley said.

"Of course," Cybil said as the nurse, Alice, approached.

"She's gone," Alice said when she reached where Tim and Ashley stood with the manager. "Such a lovely woman, taken far too soon."

"Is there … is there anything that we should know, regarding Mrs Sharp's death?" Tim asked.

"She died of natural causes," Alice informed them. "Peacefully, and in her sleep. It was how she'd hoped she'd go when it was time."

Ashley nodded as she took note of all of the people gathered around as the elderly woman's body was moved into the back of the ambulance. Among the crowd was what seemed like an equal blend of residents and staff. Ashley took her time, glancing around all of the faces. It was easy to see the level of grief on all of them. It both pleased her and saddened her that someone could have created such an emotional response in others. In their jobs, Ashley and Tim both saw so much misery caused by one human toward another. Seeing people actually care for one another was always like seeing sunshine after seeing far too much gloom.

When she was sure she'd taken note of everyone watching, she returned her focus back to the conversation beside her.

"I know it was a worrying time when she had that young man hanging around," Alice said. "But I'm glad that Sarah got to experience a little bit of joy from whatever it was that she saw in him. He wasn't here for the right reasons, but he still made her smile. What more could anyone want for such a lovely woman."

Tim smiled sadly but kept his thoughts on the

subject to himself. In his opinion, what the nurse had just said was a twisted kind of logic. Sarah Sharp had known happiness before she'd died, but she'd almost been ripped off completely - well, her family had been anyway.

As that thought passed over his mind, Tim spoke up.

"Are her kids or grandkids on their way here?" he asked.

"No," Cybil replied. "They have been notified of Sarah's passing, but none seemed to care about coming here to talk about it - not yet anyway. It is sometimes the way when we lose residents. Sometimes it takes a few days, weeks, or even months before family members come to speak to us and take away the belongings of their loved ones."

"Does this hinder your investigation in any way?" Alice asked, surprising Tim and Ashley. "Into Jeremy?"

"Our investigation is continuing," Ashley told the woman. "I do believe we have all of the information we require from your rest home, however, at least for the moment."

"I guess it doesn't matter now anyway," Alice surmised before she began to walk away. "They're both dead now."

As surprised as Tim was to hear what the nurse said before walking through the crowd, he didn't call out to her. In some ways, she was right. Whatever chapter had been evident between Sarah Sharp and the third victim, Mathew Spring - aka Jeremy Olds - it was now done with.

"Is there anything more that we can tell you to help you in your investigation, Agents?" Cybil asked, already turning her body as if to indicate that she was eager to get on with the rest of her day, preferably without any further interruptions.

"No," Ashley said. "Thank you again for letting us know."

After delivering a wave and a nod, both agents saw the rest home manager also disappear into the crowd. Turning around, they watched the ambulance begin its slow journey down the driveway. When they turned back, the crowd was already diminishing. Where a few minutes earlier, many residents and staff had stood and watched, all trying to get a better view, now there were only a handful of each.

Tim and Ashley both glanced around the people remaining, taking note of sadness on all of the faces. Once they were each sure all faces were locked into their memories, they turned to face one another.

"Let's get out of here," Tim said quietly before they began to walk towards the driveway. "I'm thankful that we know about Mrs Sharp's passing, but not sure what purpose our being summoned here served."

"Agreed," Ashley said as they climbed into the car. Once settled, ready to leave, she turned to face Tim again. "I do feel sad about Sarah though."

"It's going to happen to all of us at some stage, Ash," Tim said, feeling far more morbid than he usually did.

"True," Ashley said. "We should check with the medical examiner that her death was just due to old age."

"But what reason would someone have to kill her? The only person who could have been threatened by her at any stage was Spring, and he's dead," Tim said, surprised. Even though it would have been a natural question to ask in some cases, he hadn't even considered something unnatural had contributed to the passing of the elderly woman. "You really think someone might have killed her?"

"No," Ashley replied. "But we still need to rule it out as a possibility. She was linked to Spring, and *he* was murdered. Let's go and have a chat later on, just in case."

Hours later, Ashley and Tim were walking out into the sunshine, having spent time presenting questions to the medical examiner.

"Well, that's confirmed - definitely a death of natural causes. I'm not surprised, and I am relieved," Ashley said once out in the fresh air again. "Still needed to be sure though."

"Yeah," Tim said.

"You alright?" Ashley asked, hearing his low-energy response, which wasn't usual for him.

"Yep," Tim replied. "It gets to me sometimes, seeing bodies. I know it's part of our job, but … still … I don't know."

"At least Sarah died a peaceful death, and not at the hands of anyone else," Ashley said, encouraging a smile out of him, albeit a very sad one.

CHAPTER 30

"Okay, I'm going to print off a huge amount of stuff," Ashley said when they returned to their hotel that evening. "There's something here that I'm not seeing, and I think I'll be better able to see it if I am literally looking at it all."

Tim smiled at her. In some ways, they weren't exactly in tune when it came to investigating, but he understood what she meant. Although they didn't often want or need to produce full scale crime boards when in hotels, there was something to be said for being able to take a step or two backward and simply look at the big picture.

"Objections?" Ashley asked when she didn't receive any verbal response from him.

"None at all," Tim replied. "Printer's there, and we've got loads of paper plus reusable adhesive to safely stick stuff to this wall. You print and gather, and I'll assemble … or I can print and gather, and you assemble."

"Good plan," Ashley said, grinning.

For two hours, Ashley went through all that they'd assembled, and printed off everything she felt could be useful.

"Three victims," she finally said when she and Tim had assembled onto the wall a map that showed how everything and everyone was all related. "The biggest problem is that we still don't have much to link these guys."

"Well, we do," said Tim. "Even if we disregard that they all seemed to be catfish, using women for whatever type of financial gain they each tried to, they were still all associated with that one dating site."

"Right," Ashley agreed. "Date Today. Did we hear back from the owners of that site?"

"No, nobody is home, it would seem, but that doesn't surprise me," said Tim. "I suspect it's a site that's mostly running itself through automation."

"But someone still has to be *behind* it, right?" Ashley asked. "I mean, who developed it in the first place? Who's around to take calls if something serious happens?"

"I'll chase Tech up again to see if they can push harder for some answers," Tim said as he pulled out his phone and put through the request.

"Okay," said Ashley. "In the meantime, let's just look at this for a while. We've got Bob Masters here, with all of his victims," she added as she pointed to the long, vertical trail of paper down the left hand third of the wall. "Lance Summers here, and Mathew Spring here, with all of his aliases."

"Who's this?" Tim suddenly asked as he pointed to the printout of one Facebook page.

"Neve Cooper?" Ashley asked. "She was one of the first people we talked to, remember? She'd been catfished by..."

"Bob Masters. Yeah, I know," Tim said. "But look closer, Ash. Not at Neve, but at her contacts."

Ashley stepped forward and glanced through the small photos of the contact list they'd obtained from Neve's Facebook profile. One by one, she took some time to assess anything about them, until she finally pointed at one.

"He looks familiar," she said, squinting a little to look as closely as she could at the photo.

"He does to me, too," Tim agreed. "Come on, we need to go and talk to Neve Cooper."

"Go ... and talk to her?" Ashley asked, surprised. "Usually, you're the one suggesting we use the phone..."

"Not this time, Special Agent Ashley Power," Tim said, grinning. "Let's print off a larger copy of this profile photo, mix it up with a few of the standard random photos we keep, and see if we can learn something real interesting about this guy."

Ashley said nothing more as she watched Tim print off and grab extra papers that he wanted to use, then made his way to the door. She could see his sudden shift in energy. No matter what, that was always a good sign.

"Let's go," Tim said, feeling his adrenaline begin to flow.

CHAPTER 31

"Hope she's home," Ashley said as they once again pulled up to the home of Neve Cooper. It wasn't very much like Tim to want to move on a hunch quite so quickly, but if he was on the right track, Ashley was more than happy to let him lead the way.

"Car's there," Tim said, wondering about how he might be able to prove what he was thinking. He quickly pushed the thought aside. The more important thing he had to do was stay in the present and not get ahead of himself.

As both agents climbed out of the car, they saw the door open, and Neve appear at the door.

"I saw you pull up," she said. "Am I in trouble?"

Although surprised by the question, Tim shook his head.

"We just have a few more questions to ask you, if that's okay," he said as he and Ashley approached the woman in the doorway.

"Yeah, of course," Neve replied. "Come on in."

When all were seated, Tim pulled out the handful of pages he'd assembled at the hotel.

"We're wondering if you might be able to look through these, and let us know if anyone is familiar to you," he said, holding out the pages.

"Sure, but I already told you that I knew Bob," Neve said as she tentatively grabbed the paper. "Is there another dating site guy that something has happened to? Someone that you also think I'm chatting to?"

"Maybe," Tim replied. "If you could look through the photos please..."

He and Ashley watched as the woman in front of them took her time, shuffling the pages in her hands, looking at each photo in turn. When she reached one, she looked surprised.

"Oh," she said.

"You know him?" Tim asked, feeling his heart rate increase slightly.

"Well ... yeah ... but," Neve said, quickly putting the photo at the back of the pile and then shuffling through them all again until she was once more looking at the same face.

"Can you tell us who this is, Neve?" Ashley asked, curious.

"Yeah ... umm ... this is - well, he's not someone I've seen on a dating site, but he *looks like* a guy I went to high school with," Neve replied. "I mean, he's older in this photo, but ... it does look like him."

"You haven't seen him recently?" Tim asked.

"No," Neve said. "I haven't seen him since ... probably ... wow ... I dunno. Maybe just after we finished high school?"

"Do you have any contact with him at all?" asked Tim.

"No," Neve replied. "But ..." she added before pulling out her phone. "Is he?" she asked herself before pausing her words and appearing to scroll within her phone. "Yes! This is him," she added, holding up her phone and displaying her long list of Facebook friends. "Dean. Yes! Dean Solomon. Yeah, sorry, he is a contact in here."

"And you talk to him in there?" asked Tim.

"Um, no, I don't *think* so," Neve said as she pulled her phone back and appeared to do more scrolling.

"No, there's no record of us chatting, and I don't remember chatting to him. I accepted his friend request, obviously, but I don't think he's ever reached out and tried to actually talk to me."

"Not close friends in high school then?" Ashley asked.

"No," Neve said, chuckling. "I think he was a guy that my friends used to tease me about - a guy who liked me, or something - but we moved in different circles. Believe it or not, I was a bit cooler then," she added as a grin spread over her face. "Dean … yeah, I think he was more of a nerd, and real quiet. I'm not even sure we ever had a conversation together, to be honest."

"If you didn't chat at all, do you think there's any other way that he could have known about your online dating?" Tim asked, curious.

"Well, yeah, if he's a contact in here then he could see what's happening in my life if he follows my posts," Neve said. "I've been doing online dating for a few years now. At first, I was embarrassed, but then I thought why not share with people what I'm going through? Almost all interactions I've had with guys online, I've shared something about in my posts."

"Did you share names?" Ashley asked.

"No - well not usually," said Neve. "But now that I think about it, did I share Bob's name after he made me wary with his request for money?"

As the woman in front of them once again appeared to be scrolling up and down over her phone screen, Tim looked at Ashley. He could see that while she wasn't as sure about what they were finding out, she was getting on board with what Tim was suspecting.

"No, not his name," Neve finally said. "But this is the post I put up after that episode."

Tim accepted the phone that was handed to him, and took his time reading the post pointed out, and the comments underneath it.

"He commented," he said when he saw the name in the long list of feedback. "'Publicly shame him', he wrote here. 'Shame him, and don't give him the satisfaction of thinking he won.'"

"Oh, yeah!" Neve said. "I remember seeing that now, but then if you look through the whole lot, you'll see that lots of people said the same thing. Most told me the same thing - run! Um, so yeah, I didn't name Bob, but I did show a part of his profile photo - not the whole thing because I didn't want to cause any trouble, or get into trouble myself, but this is what other people would have seen. It's about … maybe … a *third* of his profile photo."

"And you're sure this guy - Dean - never contacted you directly, saying anything more?" Tim asked.

"Never," Neve said. "Do you think … do you think Dean has something to do with Bob's murder?"

"We're still exploring a range of possibilities," Tim replied.

"I can't imagine that he would," said Neve. "I mean, why would he? We haven't actually spoken for so many years. What … why would he? It wouldn't make any sense."

"Can we ask that you don't say anything to him, Neve?" Ashley asked. "It might be important."

"Yeah, of course," Neve said. "I wouldn't … I mean, I had no reason to contact him before this. I don't see I have any reason to now."

"Thank you," Ashley said. "Well, you have been very helpful, and we appreciate you answering our questions."

"No problem," Neve said as she stood and began walking out with Tim and Ashley. "I hope … I hope you find whoever's responsible for this. Bob might have been a cad, but being killed? That ain't cool."

"Agreed. Thank you, Neve," Tim said before he and Ashley began walking down the path.

In the car, Ashley turned to see Tim grinning.

"We got this," he said, prompting Ashley to give him a stern glance.

"We got nothing until we've got evidence, and you know it, so wind that confident butt of yours right in, Timmy Boy!" she said, making Tim laugh out loud.

"Okay," he finally said. "Back to the board?"

"Yep."

CHAPTER 32

After contemplation and looking through the different catfish victims of Lance Summers and Mathew Spring, Ashley and Tim formulated a list of people they were going to go and visit again. It seemed a long shot that one person was connected to them all, but it was possible, and definitely not something to rule out.

"We can't see Dean Solomon on the contact lists of these other victims," Ashley said as she considered several possibilities.

"And that, Partner, is exactly why we're going to talk to each of these ladies in person again," Tim said, looking far too pleased with himself as far as Ashley was concerned. "Come on."

A long while later, they'd spoken to two victims of Lance Summers. Neither had identified any of the photos that were presented to them. It was enough to produce a sliver of doubt in the minds of both agents, but not enough to stop them from continuing down the same path of questioning.

"Here we go again," Ashley said as they walked up yet another driveway, hoping the person they wanted to talk to would be home. "Don't forget that Mrs Sanders didn't want us here last time. Do you want to call her instead?"

"Nope," Tim replied.

"Oh, hi," Polly Sanders said when she opened her door and saw the agents on her doorstep.

"Is it okay for us to talk quickly, Mrs Sanders?"

Ashley asked, feeling far more patient than she could see Tim was.

"Yes, I ... I'm home alone," Polly replied. "Please come in."

"Thank you," Ashley said. Once seated, she waited for Tim to go through the same sequence of showing the photos he'd gathered.

"Would you be able to look through these and tell us if you know any of these men, please?" Tim asked as he handed the pages over.

"Oh, yes, of course," Polly said as she took the paper. Just as other women had previously, she took her time looking at each full-page photo before slipping it to the back and looking at the next one. "Oh, Dean! What's he doing in here?"

"You know Mr Solomon?" Tim asked.

"Yes, of course," Polly said, smiling although definitely with uncertainty. "Dean's been a friend of mine for many years."

"By 'friend', do you mean he's a *real life* friend of yours?" Ashley asked.

"Yes. Dean and I first met during our university years and he's been a good friend of mine ever since," Polly replied. "But why is he among these photos? Has he done something wrong? What's this about?"

"Have you seen him recently?" asked Tim.

"Yes ... well, depending on what you class as 'recently' of course. I last saw him when he and I met up for dinner about ... oh, maybe two weeks ago?" Polly said before she stood up and retrieved her phone. "Let me just check my calendar ... yes! Dean and I last had a catch up Monday before last. I haven't spoken to him since then, but that's perfectly normal. In general, we catch up in person probably once a month on average."

"Polly, is there a chance that you mentioned to him

what had happened with Lance Summers?" Ashley asked.

"Yes, he was great to talk..." Polly began to answer before seeming to consider why the question had been asked. "Please tell me you don't think Dean had something to do with what happened to Lance. Because Dean is a good man. I can't believe that he would hurt *anyone*."

"Even to protect those he cared about?" Tim asked.

"No, I don't believe so," said Polly.

"Even if he thought someone he cared about had been used and treated badly?" Tim probed.

For a moment, Polly regarded the question. Then she gave her final answer to it.

"No."

Ashley took some time to study the face of the woman before her. It was easy to sense the level of trust Polly had in the man who was quickly becoming a suspect. That didn't mean anything, of course. Most of the people who Ashley had seen convicted had had someone on their side, sure they couldn't have done what they'd done, even when a mountain of evidence said otherwise.

"Can you tell us more about the conversation that you had with him that day, Polly?" she asked. "How much did you share with him?"

"Okay," Polly replied with doubt highly audible in her voice. "Well, I'd already told him previously that I was doing the online dating thing. When we met up this last time, he asked how it was going. I told him about the whole episode with Lance - chatting to him online, meeting him in person those first few times in public, and then meeting him in the hotel room. I pretty much told him exactly what I told you last time I talked to you."

"And how did he react to that?" asked Tim.

"Oh, he was visibly upset," Polly admitted. "At first I was surprised, but when I imagined being in his shoes - hearing a friend tell the story I'd just told him - I could imagine feeling the same way."

"Did he seem angry?" Ashley asked.

"A little, but I'm sure..." Polly started to say. After taking a moment to look at the faces of both agents, she continued. "Even if he was upset, I can't believe Dean would do anything to hurt anyone, and besides, he didn't know who Lance was!"

"You didn't say his name?" asked Tim.

"No, of course not," Polly replied. "I told him what had happened, but I only talked about a guy on the internet. I didn't say Lance's name, and I didn't show my dating profile or any photo of Lance. Even if he was upset - even if he was angry about it - there's no way that he could have known who the guy *was*."

For a long while, all were quiet. In Tim's mind was the question that Polly had just presented - Dean Solomon might have been a common contact for someone that each fire victim had known, but how would he have known who the victims were?

"And you're absolutely sure that you never gave any information that could have helped Mr Solomon work it out?" he asked.

"One hundred per cent," Polly replied. "Look, Lance did what he did, and it wasn't right, but I saw it then - and still see it now - as karma for wanting to cheat on my husband. Was I angry at Lance? Sure, at the start, but then I knew *I* was the one I needed to be angry at. No matter what Lance did to me, I would never have wanted anything to happen to him, and I sure as hell wouldn't have wished him dead! So, no, I never gave out his name to anyone."

"Alright then," Tim said. "Thank you for your time."

CHAPTER 33

"Well, that's kind of looking pretty positive, I have to admit," Ashley said when they left the last residential home they'd visited. "Dean Solomon is certainly a common factor with all of these women."

"He definitely is so far, at least, but that possibility does present the question and mystery about how he found out who our victims were, and how he knew where each of them lived," Tim said. "Maybe we'll find out more once we figure out if he knew Sarah Sharp."

"Right! Let's get that done now then," Ashley said. "I keep trying to remember if his face was among the crowd we saw that last time we were at Bonnie Days. There were so many people there."

"Yeah, I thought about that too," Tim said. "He did look familiar when I looked at his photo on Neve Cooper's Facebook page. I'm just not sure if it was at the rest home that I saw him."

"One way to find out," Ashley replied as she planted her foot to the accelerator a bit more.

On approach to the rest home entrance, both agents were alert. As they walked in, they were greeted by the same receptionist that had been on duty during each of the visits Tim and Ashley had made to the building.

"Wow. Back again?" she asked, sounding far more friendly than she had the first time the agents had visited. "Can't keep away from us, huh?"

"Yeah," Tim said, delivering one of his world-class smiles. "Actually, we were hoping to speak to Mrs Douglas one more time. Is she in?"

"Yep," the receptionist said before picking up the phone and making a quick call. "She'll be here any minute."

"Agents, what can I help you with today?" they heard Cybil call out from the corridor.

"We need to speak to you one more time, if you don't mind," Ashley said.

"No, not at all," Cybil replied. "Please come through to my office."

When all were seated, she waited for Ashley or Tim to express their reason for being there.

"How can I be of assistance to you today?" she asked, prompting either agent to speak.

"Can you tell us if you know, or have seen, any of these men around here?" Tim asked, handing the same photos over that he had to several women.

"I can tell you that I know this one," Cybil said almost as soon as she began flicking through the pages. "Dean Solomon. He's one of our orderlies."

Ashley looked at Tim and saw his recognition. They had a prime suspect, and it was only a matter of time before they could prove his involvement with the horrors that had been taking place in the region.

"I assume you're here again about something more to do with Sarah Sharp," Cybil continued. "What exactly do you think Dean would have *done*?"

"Did they know each other?" Ashley asked.

"Yes, of course. All residents here are familiar with all of our staff - even the behind-the-scenes ones," Cybil said. "Dean, as an orderly, didn't assist with any nursing procedures or administration of medications, but he provided assistance to staff and residents in many other ways."

"And how have you found him ... as a person?" Tim asked.

"He's a lovely young man," Cybil replied. "Always polite, always on time, and the residents rave about him. I've never heard anyone speak badly about him during his years here."

"How well do *you* know him? Do you think he's capable of hurting someone?" Tim dared to ask.

"I ... don't ... *think* ... so," Cybil said. "Then again, do we ever really know anyone?" She paused for a long while before continuing. "I only see what I see of my staff, here at work, and I don't think any manager ever fully sees the true nature of their workers. I'm really not qualified to speak about what they're like outside of here. And Dean - well, like I say, I've had no reason to be unhappy with his work here, so, to be honest, I really haven't had much to do with him."

"Sure, but what *can* you tell us about him?" Tim asked.

"As a staff member?" Cybil asked. "He has always been a hard worker, and like I said, he gets on well with the residents."

"And other staff members?" asked Ashley.

"I've never had any complaints from anyone about him, including other staff members," said Cybil. "As far as I know, he's just a nice guy who quietly does a good job."

"Do you know anything about his life outside of here?" Tim asked.

"No, not really," Cybil replied. "I don't know him on a personal level, but you're welcome to talk to other members of the staff about this. There is a small staffroom here, so if anyone got to know him personally, that might be where they'd do it." She paused as she looked at her watch. "It's almost dinner time now so..." she started to say before appearing to look at something on her computer screen. "Dean only works day shift so has already finished for the day, but there will be other staff members in the staffroom right now, and they might be able to help with your questions. I can take you down there if you like."

"Yes, that would be great," Ashley replied. "Thank you."

"Agents," she heard Cybil call out after she'd left them in the corridor to the staffroom. When Ashley turned around, she could read the expression of concern on the rest home manager's face. "If there is anything that is of concern about my staff member, I trust that you will tell me immediately. We take pride in caring for our residents. If someone is among us that can't be trusted to act in their best interest..."

"If anything is determined, we'll let you know," Tim reassured her. "Thank you."

Resuming their walk toward the staffroom, both agents saw a familiar face walk out of what appeared to be an adjoining locker room.

"Oh! Hello!" Alice Brown said as she started to breeze past. "Back again, I see..." she called out.

"Actually, Mrs Brown, can we ask you a quick question or two?" Tim called back to her and saw her halt in her progress.

"I have to rush home...kids!" the nurse started to say as she edged further away from the agents.

"We can walk out with you," Ashley said. "It'll only take a minute," she added and was pleased to see Alice stop and paste on a smile.

"Are you able to tell us if an orderly here - Dean - Solomon - was close with Sarah?" Tim asked.

"Oh, yes, those two - they'd talk all day if Dean didn't need to get on with his work," Alice said, for the moment looking annoyed at the subject. "What's this about? Has he done something wrong?"

"Oh, no, we are still working our way through our investigation," Tim replied.

"Into the death of that man ... Jeremy..." Alice suggested.

"Yes," said Ashley. "Is there anything about Dean that you think might be helpful to our investigation?"

"Something about Dean? No, he's a nice guy," said Alice, still attempting to edge closer to the exit. "He's great with the residents here, and I think he does volunteer firefighting in his off-hours, so I'm guessing he's a caring person all round. What other kind of person would work a full time job, and then go and work another shift for free somewhere else? Sorry but I really do have to run ... family obligations."

Ashley and Tim watched as the woman removed herself completely, not looking back. When Ashley turned to face Tim, she suspected his face mirrored her own.

"Firefighter," Tim said quietly.

"Yep," Ashley agreed. "Let's see if anyone else around here has some information to offer about Mr Dean Solomon."

Half an hour later, Tim and Ashley were back in the car, eager to move on to find out more about the man they now believed to be the main suspect in the deaths of all three victims.

"Head back to North Road Fire Department again?" Tim asked. "He might actually be down there if he works those shifts around the ones he does here," he added as he glanced at his watch.

"Good idea," Ashley agreed. She felt motivated, and she felt invigorated. Nothing was final yet, but she felt sure they were at least on the right path.

CHAPTER 34

As they had with so many people throughout the day, Tim and Ashley handed over the photographs of the same few men, then sat quietly as they watched Captain John Rogers glance through them.

"This … this is one of my guys," he finally said, pointing at the same face that others had identified. "Volunteer. Dean Solomon."

"Do you know anything about him, John?" Ashley asked. "Maybe, what he does outside of his work hours with the station?"

"He works at the local rest home," John replied. "He's worked there for longer than he's been here. I think it was actually through a connection there that he became a fire fighter with us in the first place. Nice guy. Seems pretty dedicated to being a *good* fire fighter. Takes instruction well, and just gets on with it. I've never heard any complaints about him. Why are you asking about him? I'm guessing you don't think he's got anything to do with this series of explosions."

"You sound certain," Tim said.

"About Dean?" John asked, prompting Tim to nod in reply. "He's a good kid. There's never been any issue reported to me about him - not from the staff here, or from anyone from the local community. He treats everyone well. I've never heard a bad word come from his mouth. If you're thinking he's got something to do with hurting people, you can't be on the right track. I just don't believe it."

Ashley studied his face for a long while. He was convincing in his plea of innocence for one of his staff, but was that all it was? An employer being protective over a member of their staff?

"Does Mr Solomon have a shift tonight?" she asked, then waited patiently as John delivered a long non-wavering glance before he finally answered.

"Yes," John said. "He's on the six o'clock shift. He's always early, so I'd say he'll be here within the next thirty minutes."

"We can wait for him," Ashley said and saw the man across from her nod, all the while looking concerned.

"Sure," John said. "He usually parks in the carpark out back, and heads in the back door to where the engines are."

"Thank you," Tim said as he stood, having received a look from Ashley that he interpreted to mean it was time for them to leave.

Walking out of the office, once again the agents stopped and looked at the staff photos.

"He's not there," Ashley said. "I didn't see him on the rest home staff wall either."

"Shy guy?" Tim suggested. "Or maybe he just likes to stay under the radar. Orderly at a rest home, and volunteer fire fighter - both jobs that might not be highlighted enough to get onto walls like this in these places."

"True," Ashley agreed. "Let's move the car so we can sit and wait while watching the car park. It'd be good to see him as soon as he arrives for his shift."

Inside the car, Ashley found herself pondering what they'd been told by not one but two workplaces.

"All of the people who've spoken about him don't seem to think he's capable of hurting anyone," she said.

"Yeah, they're all pretty certain he's just a nice guy," said Tim. "Then again, we've met quite a few people who were liked by all of the people who knew them, but then turned out to be nasty as. Look at our victims themselves. All of the people we spoke to at the hospital about Bob Masters, talked as if the guy was an angel, but he was consciously trying to rip off women online."

"Plus the suspicion that he might have been stealing from the hospital," Ashley added.

"Exactly!" said Tim. "Everyone might love this guy, Dean Solomon. That doesn't mean he didn't kill three people so far."

"So far?" Ashley asked, shuddering as she pulled into a suitable spot to sit and wait. The thought of more fires - and more bodies - wasn't a good one. "We need to find this guy before he takes on a fourth victim."

"And we will," Tim reassured her. "We're on his tail now."

"Tim, you know that this one will be hard to prove, even if this guy *is* the killer," Ashley said. "Proof. *Evidence*. How are we going to find that?"

"Yeah, I know," said Tim. "Don't worry. We'll..." he continued before he saw the suspect enter his vision. "There," he added with a nod of his head.

When Ashley glanced to where Tim was indicating, she saw Dean Solomon climbing out of the car he'd just parked. Choosing to let him get inside the building before they approached him, Ashley and Tim remained where they were. Once they saw him pass through the back entrance to the large structure, they moved.

CHAPTER 35

As they entered the building, the agents moved around the large fire trucks until they had Dean Solomon in their sights. Moving closer to where he stood, talking and smiling with a couple of other fire fighters, they could see the moment when he saw them. Both agents were prepared for him to run.

Before they reached him, they were surprised by the movement of another fire fighter looking directly at them and then immediately start to walk briskly away. As Tim and Ashley happened to glance at Dean, and see him looking at his work colleague with a blend of surprise and amusement, they both looked in the direction of the man who'd left. The way that he glanced at Dean and the agents was enough to inspire Tim to move quickly after him.

As he did, Ashley grew aware of Dean Solomon having shifted his attention to her. She'd thought he might try and get away once he suspected law enforcement was walking right toward him. She was surprised that his stance didn't change, and he didn't move away at all, instead looking at her with an open expression of simple curiosity.

"Is Stan in trouble?" he asked. "I haven't seen him run that far or fast *ever* - even when we've been attending a fire!"

"Stan...?" Ashley asked, her curiosity and then doubt increasing by the minute.

"Brown," Dean replied, grinning. "Nice guy, but a

bit weird sometimes. Helped get me the job here, though, so I kind of owe him, in a way."

"I see," Ashley said, processing what she was being told. "And how do you know Mr Brown, if you don't mind me asking?"

"Oh, I work with his wife - Alice," Dean said.

"At...?"

"Bonnie Days," Dean replied. "It's a rest home…"

"Yes, we've been there recently," Ashley said. "I'm sure you know we were there when Mrs Sharp was taken away."

"No, sorry," Dean said. "That was my day off and, to be honest, I'm kind of glad. She was a lovely old lady, Sarah. She never looked down on me even once during the time we were both there, even though I'm just an orderly. Always wanted to take the time to tell me stories about her life. She had some *amazing* stories to tell! Yes, it was sad when I learned she'd passed, but it's one of the things I've had to get used to working there. It's a bit like Hotel California, you know - you can check in but you'll never leave. Not alive anyway. It's a fact of life, I know, but it's always hard when one of them goes."

"Were you aware of the man that Sarah was seeing?" Ashley asked. In response, she heard him scoff.

"Seeing - yeah, right," Dean replied. "When she told me she had some young guy coming around, it was sad enough, but she seemed happy, you know. When she told me that she was thinking of changing her will, I couldn't just sit back and do nothing."

"So what did you do?" Ashley asked, wondering if she was about to get a confession.

"Went straight to the boss and made sure she knew what was going on," Dean said. "She said she was welcoming of my concern, but then just basically said that it was up to Sarah if she wanted to leave all of her estate to him - could leave it all to a *cat*, if she wanted to. The boss didn't *not* care, but she really didn't seem to care either." He paused for a long while before speaking again. "Alice, on the other hand," he began as he smiled and scoffed.

"What about Alice?" Ashley asked.

"She was *way* at the other extreme," said Dean. "The more I told her about what I knew about that guy, and that I thought he was leading Sarah on to get at her money, the angrier Alice got. I mean, I didn't want to see Sarah get ripped off by anyone, let alone an idiot like that, but I was surprised by Alice's over-the-top reaction to everything she and I had both been told by Sarah."

"Do you get on well with Alice, Mr Solomon?" Ashley asked, eager to pursue a new line of consideration.

"Most of the time, yeah," Dean said. "I mean, she did go a bit strange after all of that episode."

"Strange, how?" asked Ashley.

"Hmm, I guess ... until then, she'd always been open and friendly toward me," Dean replied. "After we both knew that Sarah might have been led on by some guy, Alice ... I don't know ... she seemed to become ... *aloof* might be the word? Like she'd wanted to know me before then, but definitely wanted to keep her distance from me after that - almost as if she didn't want anyone to see that she knew me."

"Was that after Sarah started talking about the man?" Ashley asked. "Or after the man died?"

"Oh, yeah, I remember that day," Dean said. "Well, I wasn't at work on that day that the news arrived at the rest home, but the next day I was at work, I saw Sarah and she was pretty upset. I'd actually thought she was pretty much over him by then, because she'd stopped talking about him. Seeing her upset all over again after she'd heard of his death was heart breaking. She was such a lovely woman. Always reminded me of my grandma."

"Can I ask, Alice's husband…"

"Stan."

"Yes, has he also acted differently toward you since the death of the man Sarah had been seeing?" Ashley asked.

"Oh, yeah, a bit, but he's always a bit strange, old Stan is," Dean said, smiling sadly. "It was weird. He seemed nice at the start, helping me with getting some volunteer work here and all that. But yeah, I guess his level of friendliness toward me has changed a bit as time's gone on. Was it around that time? Hmm, maybe. I dunno. We don't often get shifts together. Most days, like today, he's leaving his shift just as I'm arriving, so our paths don't cross all that often."

As absorbed as she was in what she was hearing, Ashley gave thought to Tim. It had been a few minutes since he'd taken off in pursuit of the man who'd begun to run when he'd seen Tim and Ashley. Glancing at Dean again, she knew she couldn't yet dismiss him as a suspect, but her analysis of the entire situation had definitely taken a sharp turn.

"We are going to need to speak to you again, Mr Solomon," she said as she began to walk away. "Don't leave town."

"Yeah, no problem," Dean said, smiling with a clear expression of uncertainty on his face. "I'm not hard to find. Generally I'm here most evenings, and at Bonnie Days most days."

"Thank you," Ashley said. She'd been sure he'd been the initiator of all three gas explosions and the deaths of three men. As she walked away from him, her gut feeling no longer lay with him at all.

CHAPTER 36

"Why do you think your wife would do anything like that?" Tim asked the man he'd cornered, just as Ashley approached. When he turned and saw her, he could see that she'd also begun to question what they'd thought to be true. "Mr Brown, why do you think your wife would want to hurt anyone?"

Ashley remained quiet as she approached where the two men stood. She had no idea what information Tim had just gained from the man in front of them, but it was clear that Stan Brown wasn't quick-witted enough to even try to get away from the agent who'd stopped him from leaving.

"She ... she's *obsessed*!" Stan Brown said. "Ever since her mother left everything to a guy that she hardly knew, Alice ... Alice has just been so angry, *all the time*!"

"Angry about her mother's estate going to someone other than her?" Tim asked.

"No! Yes! I..." Stan began to say. "She's my wife, and I love her to death, but when that all happened, something snapped inside of her. I don't know how she found out that this guy was intentionally ripping her mother off. I don't know *anything* except that my wife is no longer the same person that I married. She was always so loving and so giving. Now ... sometimes, now, I feel like I don't even know who she is anymore. Don't get me wrong. I do still love her..."

"But you suspect she's hurt people?" Ashley asked,

knowing she was only hearing the tail end of a much bigger conversation.

"Maybe," Stan said, his voice revealing a level of self-defeat. "To be honest, I'm really not sure. She hasn't said anything definite to me - she hasn't *told* me anything - but a while back..."

"A while back, what?" Tim prompted when he saw the man falter in whatever it was that he'd been intending to say.

"A while back, she asked me ... she asked me about gas lines," Stan finally admitted. "At first, I thought she was being silly, asking questions like she was."

"Did you suspect her having had something to do with these fires and deaths, after that first explosion?" Tim asked.

"No," Stan said, shaking his head. "Honestly, I didn't even give it a thought. By then, the conversation we'd had was in the past and I'd forgotten all about it. It was later, when she mentioned something in passing ... something about a woman at the rest home having been saved from making the same mistake Alice's mother did ... I can't remember exactly what she said, but something about what she was saying - the words she used - made me think that the woman in the rest home was somehow associated with the last guy who'd died in these explosions. When I thought that, I wondered..."

Both agents remained quiet as they glanced at each other, and then at the man before them. It was easy to see devastation on his face. While he'd looked guilty when he'd run out of the station, Ashley and Tim both wondered if he could have had anything to do with the three explosions.

"We saw Alice leaving the rest home a little while ago, Mr Brown," Ashley said. "Do you know where she would have been heading? Would she be going home?"

"Yes," Stan said. Still, he made no attempt to move. "She might stop somewhere to pick something up on the way home, but as far as I know, she has nothing on that would mean she isn't heading back to the house."

"I'll arrange for backup," Ashley said to Tim before gaining the Brown home address from Stan, and then walking away to make the call. "Don't let him go anywhere, and don't let him use his phone."

A short phone call later, she returned.

"They're on their way to the house," she said. "They'll meet us there."

"Time to take a ride, Mr Brown," Tim said.

"My car…"

"Will be safe here, I'm sure."

CHAPTER 37

"Stan?" Ashley and Tim heard Alice call out when she opened the door to her home, and saw her husband standing behind them. "What's going on?"

"We'd like you to go with these officers for questioning, please, Alice," Ashley said as she pointed to the supporting local law enforcement officers.

"Stan?" Alice asked again, focusing only on her husband.

"You need to go, Alice," Stan said. "You need help. This has been going on for too long."

"No," Alice said, trying to struggle away from the two officers who'd flanked her. "No! Stan! What have you done?! Stan!" she yelled out. "Stan! Don't let them do this to me!"

As the interaction between husband and wife unfolded, Tim watched both closely. Until evidence was found, he knew Stan and Alice could both be considered suspects, just as he knew Dean Solomon could still be regarded as one as well. One person naming another in a crime didn't mean anything. It could be the truth. It could also be a case of someone trying to make another person look guilty, to deflect away from their own part in a crime.

"Take him separately," he said, nodding at another officer as he pointed to Stan. "We won't be far behind."

"Dean?" Ashley asked when they were alone again. "Bring him in too?"

"Let's see what these guys tell us in a formal interview," Tim suggested. "Either someone's going to tell all…"

"Or all are going to lie."

CHAPTER 38

Hours later, after Tim had been in touch with the tech team and asked them to urgently facilitate delving extensively into the computer activities of Dean Solomon and Alice and Stan Brown, he and Ashley sat inside an interrogation room. Facing them was Alice Brown. She wasn't the only person they'd be interviewing, but she was the first.

"Stan has already told us he thinks it was you who made three gas explosions happen, Alice," Tim said.

"Why would you do that, Alice?" Ashley asked, leaning toward the suspect. "You work in a rest home. You work around elderly people who are vulnerable. According to your employer, you're a dedicated worker. You work in a *caring* role. How could you hurt people in this way?"

For a long while, Alice sat and stared at both agents, appearing to shift between feeling bold and defiant, determined to not say anything, but then seeming defeated and not wanting to put up a fight at all.

"I haven't hurt anyone," she stated, her tone aligned with a decision to go with defiance rather than defeat. "Me? No. Dean. Dean Solomon. He's the one you're after. You should be interviewing him! I always knew there was something weird about him. The way that he cozied up to Sarah and the other elderly women in the rest home. It's not right. It's just creepy all round."

After listening to the spiel that sounded

impassioned, even if it might not be related to reality, Ashley glanced at Tim. In truth, they both knew they couldn't be sure who was being honest and who was lying among the three people they'd spoken to. Before they could embark on further questioning of the woman in front of them, a knock on the door alerted them to news.

As Tim stepped out, Ashley studied the woman in front of her. Someone who'd dedicated her entire working life to caring for others. How could someone like that be a killer? It made no sense to Ashley, but she knew that history told many stories of people just like that - people in roles where they appeared to care for people and want them to live, while quietly killing them instead. It was one of the many sad situations that demonstrated just how horribly human beings could treat each other.

After a couple of minutes, Tim stepped back into the room and sat down again.

"As much as you want to deny what you've done, Alice, we have found evidence of you stalking - and cyber stalking - each of the victims."

"I don't know what you mean!" Alice said with a level of passion in her voice that greatly contrasted the increasing level of desperate panic in her eyes. "I'm a nurse. How would I know how to ... I don't even know what cyber stalking *is*!"

"I have printouts right here," Tim said as he laid pages on the table. "These are evidence that you saw, and were watching at great length, the dating profiles of Bob Masters, Lance Summers, and Mathew Spring, aka Jeremy Olds. I believe it would be highly coincidental that you were watching them like you were, but had nothing to do with the accidents that claimed their lives."

"I didn't talk to *any* of those people!" Alice

screamed. "I'm happily married. Why would I be on any dating sites? I love my husband. I'd never cheat on him." She paused for a long time, as if waiting to see if any of her words might be chipping away at any soft side of the agents she faced. "I love my husband!"

"Yes, we can see that," Tim said as he produced another page. "From the information we've been able to gather, we don't think that you had any affair behind your husband's back. From what we've read, we also don't believe that you intended to. You did, however, assemble quite a considerable amount of evidence for us that supports what we believe - screen shots of each of these victims' dating profiles and photos; plus photos of the victims entering their homes on different days. Seems you not only were watching them online from a quiet distance, but you were also watching all three of these victims in real life."

"*Victims*?!" Alice asked, her tone changing again. "They aren't victims! The *victims* are the women that these men used, over and over again. It's always the way with your type, isn't it," she added, looking from one agent to the other. "Always, you see the women as being the ones who are responsible for whatever happens to them. You think that women like those on dating sites should *expect* to be ripped off. You think that if they're in there, they deserve whatever happens to them."

"No, Alice. That isn't true at all," Ashley said. "Nobody should be treated the way that the women we've spoken to were, but that doesn't change what you have the right to do about it. You killed three people..."

"Three people who had to be stopped!" Alice exclaimed. "If I hadn't stopped them, they would have kept going, making a mockery of more and more women. It's just not right that they can do that to people ... people who just want to find love! They had to be stopped!"

The passion that Alice seemed to feel about the subject was evident to Tim and Ashley. Even so, both agents sat back and waited as they let Alice assemble her thoughts, and tell whatever she wanted to tell. While she'd begun with denying she had anything to do with the explosions and resulting deaths, it wasn't long before she was telling all, and then signing a confession.

"They killed her," she said quietly when she'd stopped writing and pushed the pad and pen back across the table.

"Who?" Ashley asked, surprised by the words she'd just heard.

"My sister - Stacey," Alice replied, not hiding the misery on her face. "After our mother died and we found out that she'd left everything to a man we didn't even know, my sister was devastated. She always thought she wasn't good enough to be loved, and these guys proved that to her."

Not understanding what she was talking about, Tim asked her for clarity. While the initial interview had appeared to be moving along easily, with Alice speaking well, the more she spoke, the more her words seemed garbled. It took time before the message she was trying to get across to Ashley and Tim, finally began to make some sense to them.

"Our mother discovered online dating a few months before she left us," Alice said. "We didn't even know it had happened. She said nothing about it, even though she did give us a hint a couple of times, implying that she might have met someone new. We were glad for her when we realized that. She'd always been a loving mother to us, and she deserved to be loved and in a new relationship. But over time, every time we thought we were going to meet the guy, it didn't happen. He'd tell her that he was keen to meet us, but then he *always* seemed to have an excuse about why it couldn't happen that time. After a while, we assumed it might have all been in our mother's imagination," she added. "I'm ashamed to say it, but my sister and I thought our mother must have been misreading something. We thought that it was likely she liked someone and was overvaluing the attention she was receiving from a man who was only being friendly to her and didn't have any romantic intentions toward her at all.

"When my mother died, and the will was read, it was so … *unbelievable* that we didn't know what to do," Alice continued. "After extensive talks with various lawyers, we knew nothing could be done to change anything. Our mother had left everything to him, and there was nothing we could do about it."

"And that made you angry," Tim surmised.

"Of course I was angry!" Alice exclaimed. "Angry, but also determined to just get on with life. I hadn't been living with anything of my mother's before she left us, so there was no reason why my life would be any different after she passed."

"And Stacey?" Ashley asked.

"Stacey took it much harder than I did," Alice replied. "All throughout her life, she'd believed she couldn't be loved. We all told her that wasn't true, and that if she could just get out and be amongst people more often, we were sure she'd meet someone," Alice said. "Then she said she thought she *had* found someone. The day she told us that, was a happy day. My sister had thought she'd found *love*, but that person ended up being someone who just wanted to use her. They'd heard Stacey talking about our mother having died, and the guy wanted her to try and get her share of any estate that she could. When Stacey said it was over and done with, and there would be no money coming her way, the guy told her he didn't want to see her anymore. Severed ties with her and left her hanging - just like that."

For a long while, she remained quiet as Tim and Ashley just watched and waited for whatever she was going to add.

"That was Stacey's breaking point," Alice said as her eyes began to water. "A week after that, I received news that my sister had taken her own life," she added, her voice breaking as she began to weep. "These men - they took everything from my mother, and then they took everything from me, by making my sister kill herself."

"I'm very sorry for your loss, Alice," Ashley said. "You and your family have been through a lot."

"Because of *them*!" Alice exclaimed, her boldness returning.

"Just to be clear, Alice," Tim said. "Were Bob Masters, Lance Summers, or Mathew Spring, the men who hurt your mother and/or your sister? Were they the men they were speaking to?"

"Not them, but they're just the same!" Alice said. "They're *all* the same! These guys are making it their *job* to lure women in, make them fall in love with them, and then take them for all that they're worth. It's not fair!"

"No, it's not," Ashley said, feeling surprisingly sorry for the woman. "Even so, Alice, the wrong that these men have done doesn't give you the right to have done the wrong that *you* have."

"What is your husband's involvement in this?" Tim asked, wondering if the woman facing them was being honest in her appearance of being defeated. It was always interesting to watch people they interviewed. Body language and facial expression told a much greater story than words ever did.

"Nothing," Alice replied. "I asked him how gas works, but that's all. He didn't ask me why I wanted to know, and I didn't tell him. Stan has nothing to do with any of this."

"And Dean Solomon?" Ashley asked, curious about whether the young man who everyone had only spoken highly about, could still have anything to do with anything that had happened.

"No," Alice said. "Dean is just a young guy who I thought could be blamed if it looked like I might be a suspect. He had nothing at all to do with any of this. He's just a guy who truly cares about the elderly we tend to, and he cared about Sarah. When he told me a few times that he had one friend or another - women - who were also going through being used online, I thought..."

"You thought he might be the perfect person to take the fall for the murders that you committed," Ashley suggested and saw Alice nod in response.

"Dean had nothing to do with this," Alice said. "He was just a pawn in a game that only I played."

"Not much of a game when people get killed," Tim said, not feeling at all sorry for the woman he faced.

Resolved that Alice wasn't likely to say anything that was going to get her husband in trouble, or blame anyone else at all for any involvement in what she'd done, Tim listened to the small amount more that she wanted to say, and then shut the interview down.

They had a spoken confession on tape, and they had a written confession as well. It wouldn't be something to be relied upon, but they also had evidence of a digital nature that showed the extent to which Alice had been stalking all three victims before they died. It wouldn't be as strong a case if she turned around and said she wasn't guilty at a later date, but it was a sound start.

CHAPTER 39

"I feel quite drained after all that," Ashley admitted when she and Tim later settled into the car for the long journey back to their individual lives of normality. Following their interview with Alice, they'd watched her be taken away, showing in her expression that she was resigned to her fate. With enough hours left in the day, Tim and Ashley had decided to head home. There was nothing more to be found out for the case.

As Tim fastened his seatbelt in preparation for their long drive home, he glanced at Ashley. Usually, she was at least a little bit upbeat after finishing an investigation. As he studied her face, he could see she'd been more affected by the case than he'd seen her be after other ones they'd worked on together. Perhaps it was because they rarely investigated deaths, or perhaps it was due to another reason altogether.

"You're quiet. What's on your mind, Ash?" he quietly asked, prompting her to let out whatever thoughts appeared to be plaguing her at that moment.

"Not sure, to be honest," Ashley replied as she looked at him and started the engine. "I think this has just been one of those annoying cases where I can see the reasoning behind why the perpetrator did what they did."

"It happens now and then," Tim said, nodding. "But the law…"

"Is the law," Ashley said as Tim did, resulting in them both laughing.

Tim smiled at her, appreciating the moment Ashley's mood had changed from her looking almost despondent, to smiling and happy again. He loved when that happened. If he had his way, his partner would always be happy and positive. It was an unfortunate aspect of their job that there was so often so much that didn't contribute to happy thoughts. All cases provided their fair share of concern, seriousness, and a need for someone's behavior to be called out and stopped - even the ones that didn't result in someone's death.

"Right," Ashley said as she veered the car out onto the road. "Let's get you home so you can have some privacy, peace and quiet. I know you love that so much," she added as she delivered to him a wink.

Tim chuckled.

"You and I both know that it's not *me* that needs privacy, peace and quiet after a case is finished, Ash," he teased her.

"Oh, yeah," Ashley said as she grinned. "You're right. That's me."

Hours later, after she pulled up outside of Tim's apartment, Ashley waited for him to grab his bag. On occasion, dropping him home after an investigation had ended had been the moment when he'd wanted to talk to her about something serious. She couldn't tell from his current demeanor if he was going to try it again that day or not.

"Enjoy your time off, Partner," Tim said, quietly determined to not spoil their relaxed drive home by yet again telling her how he was feeling. "See you back at work!"

Ashley smiled at him. She'd not wanted him to say anything serious to her. She should have been glad that he didn't seem to want to. She wasn't sure she was.

"Bye, Tim!" she called out as he closed the door. As she veered out onto the road, she glanced in the rear vision mirror and saw him standing where he was, not appearing to be in any hurry to get inside his home. It took some effort for Ashley to refocus and move her sight to the road again and put her partner right out of her mind, at least for a few days.

CHAPTER 40

As he stood on the footpath and watched Ashley's car pull away, Tim took a moment to take note of his feelings. He was always emotional when a case ended. That was just one of the many ways that he and Ashley were so different. Whenever a case had been solved, Tim felt like he needed to be close to someone. In contrast, the only thing Ashley seemed to need when a case had been solved was solitude. It hadn't taken long for Tim to realize that on those days, being around someone seemed to be the absolute *last* thing that his partner wanted.

Yes, in many ways they were alike, but they were also very different. Knowing that always left him feeling equally happy that they were partners who worked so well together, and sad that they were work partners and not anything more.

As he picked up his bag and turned to approach his home, he smiled to himself. In several other similar moments - those after a case ended - he'd begun to express to Ashley just how highly he regarded her. On each of those occasions, he'd been able to easily sense that she hadn't wanted him to say anything. More than once, he'd gotten only as far as opening his mouth to express how he was feeling, before Ashley had pleaded with him to not say anything. It had become a well-rehearsed routine that both of them had come to rely upon every time a case was completed.

This time, he'd held back from telling her he

wanted to chat. Had he wanted to say something to her? Yes. Had he silently considered what he *could* say to her? Yes. But had he spoken? No. Not this time. This time, he'd chosen to put her wishes ahead of his own. She didn't want any emotional stuff from him. She wanted nothing at all from him except his professional work ethic. That was nothing to be saddened by. They worked well together, and when they were working, they got on well enough. It wasn't all that he'd have loved to have explored with her, but it was enough. It was *more* than enough.

Allowing himself to feel the combination of happiness and a sliver of sadness over that as he put his key in the door, he then pushed the sadness away. He had an amazing job that he loved. In that job, he had an amazing partner who he loved to work alongside. In almost everything that he wanted in life, he was blessed and he was lucky.

Almost everything.

CHAPTER 41

As always whenever she got home after the completion of an investigation, Ashley closed her front door, dumped her overnight case in the foyer of her apartment, and then walked into her bedroom. Once there, she lay down on her bed, fully clothed, and breathed deeply. She loved doing all aspects of her job, but there was something intensely therapeutic about returning to her home - her safe haven away from the criminals of the world - and focusing on pushing it all from her mind.

Sometimes when she got home after an investigation ended, she felt invigorated - revved up in the happiness she felt that she'd played a part in trying to get justice for a victim. At other times, she felt like she currently did. There was still happiness in knowing she'd done her job, and done it well. But she was also aware that there was a growing restlessness inside of her. What did it mean? Was it time to hang up her hat and move on to a new chapter in her career life? Was it time to take a long holiday and forget about her work completely for a while?

Whatever was driving her restlessness, she knew that her emotions had been switched on by investigating the deaths of three people. They might not have been the best people on the planet, but they were people, and they'd been killed. It proved yet again that life could be cut short at any time. That made her all the more determined to actually get out and live … right after a nap.

After such a thought, Special Agent Ashley Power finally slept. Any more thinking could be left for another day … and another case.

186

The End

<hr>

OTHER BOOKS
BY
ANN M PRATLEY

<hr>

A POWER MOORE INVESTIGATION TALE
HOONIGAN
ANN M PRATLEY

HOONIGAN

Tristan Clarkson has woken up, over and over, bound to a chair and unable to see. He has no idea where he is, or why he is in the situation he's woken to. His memory is vague, protecting him from recent events that will eventually haunt him for the rest of his life. He wants to remember, but at the same time his mind acts as though he really, really doesn't. Initially he's confused. With each waking, his memory clears that little bit more, as do his senses. He soon becomes aware that the very person who has abducted him, is in the room with him, determined to make Tristan pay for something he cannot even remember.

Meanwhile, in a hospital nearby a patient has been taken. With the help of Special Agents Ashley Power and Tim Moore, an investigation begins into where the man has been taken, and who would have reason to remove him. With the patient having already been weak from time in a coma, time is of the essence in finding him alive.

Hoonigan is a blend of crime and suspense, intermingled with the strength of friendship, and the awakening of one father's realization of just how much his son really means to him.

A POWER MOORE INVESTIGATION TALE

RESOLUTION
of
HAPPINESS

ANN M PRATLEY

RESOLUTION OF HAPPINESS

Fiona Thompson - better known as Flo to everyone who knew her - took a plunge and stepped out of her comfort zone and into the world of online dating.

With persistence she found her prince.
He ticked all the boxes.
He was handsome.
He was financially secure.
He loved her.
He married her.

She was warned by friends and family that there was something off about him. She didn't listen.

Then she woke up cold, inside the darkness of a wooden box.

Join Special Agents Ashley Power and Tim Moore as they investigate the disappearance of Flo, going on a surprising journey that nobody in Flo's world could possibly anticipate.

A POWER MOORE INVESTIGATION TALE
HOME BY THE SEA
ANN M PRATLEY

HOME BY THE SEA

A decade ago, homeless people began disappearing from four neighboring towns. Day to day, the commuters making their way to and from work never took notice of the less fortunate they passed. They didn't notice as the number of homeless reduced. They didn't even notice when entire groups of homeless people vanished.

A young woman, eager to find out where her grandfather disappeared to, began trying to find him. When four police departments dismissed her, telling her that her grandfather would no doubt turn up when he wanted to, she was too young to realize she should pursue the matter further.

Now, ten years on, she's stepped up and pushed harder for something to be done to find not only her grandfather but also the countless other people who seemed to have disappeared around the same time.

Called in to investigate the disappearances, Special Agents Ashley Power and Tim Moore find themselves searching for - and finding - so much more than they thought they would.

A POWER MOORE INVESTIGATION TALE

TIGER
IN OUR
HOUSE

ANN M PRATLEY

TIGER IN OUR HOUSE

When Alana Templeton goes to do the simple task of hanging her laundry outdoors, she becomes aware that something is not as it should be in her yard. The sound she hears is one that many people might not recognize at first. For Alana, it is, surprisingly, a sound she's heard before.

Being in the yard, with her toddler in the doorway of their home, she knows the right thing to do is whatever she can to save him. The previous time, she succeeded, but will she this time?

A woman and her infant being put in danger of being attacked by the large animal that has escaped the local wildlife park, prompts an investigation into whether there might be more than just bad luck behind the two events. It seems unlikely that someone could have used such a beast for an attempt on someone's life. Then again, it seems unlikely that the animal would escape its confine and end up at the same location two times in a row.

Called in to figure out what might be behind the strange occurrences, Special Agents Ashley Power and Tim Moore begin to delve into an elaborate and rather unconventional scheme to hurt someone through an act of revenge.

ALESSANDRA
(CHISHOLM MANOR SERIES - BOOK #1)

Great passion can come from great innocence…

After receiving news from her parents of a possible betrothal, Alessandra, an 18 year old with an ingrained belief that no-one would ever wish to marry her, finds herself in a love so great that at times she cannot breathe. Married to someone as inexperienced as herself, she finds herself on a sexual journey of learning and exploration.

The combination of their mutual inexperience contributes to Alessandra discovering a degree of emotional and physical love that she has never before realized could exist.

That love will be tested by someone from her past with sinister intentions. Jealous of the physical love Alessandra shares with her husband, he is set on doing whatever it takes to have the woman he desires, no matter the cost.

ELIZABETH
(CHISHOLM MANOR SERIES - BOOK #2)

When innocence and scoundrel collide…

When Elizabeth Chisholm visits Venice with her family, she is unexpectedly drawn to Lord Byron - a man eleven years her senior. What she sees him present to her is grace, gentlemanlike behaviour, and an enthusiasm to pursue her. What she doesn't see is how much of a scoundrel he is - something he can easily hide from a mind and a heart as pure as hers.

Having grown up watching the deep and intense love of her parents - Alessandra and Edward - Elizabeth does all that is asked of her day to day but, now the age of eighteen, deeply yearns for someone to love her. The attention she receives from the handsome lord nicely fits into her desires, but where does she fit into his?

As Elizabeth is lured into the ongoing uncertainty of Lord Byron's attention, a young Scotsman wants to overcome his intense shyness. The love of art is something that he shares with Elizabeth, but he knows he can't compete with the confidence and handsomeness of the English lord.

At the request of Elizabeth's brother, Charles, the young Scotsman proves his worth by attempting to draw Elizabeth away as more things are learned about Lord Byron's actions across Europe, but is it too late? Is the reputation of Elizabeth Chisholm already sealed and irreparable, just through being associated with the scandalous English gentleman?

FREEDOM
OF
FLIGHT
CHRISTIAN
ANN M PRATLEY

FREEDOM
OF
FLIGHT
BRANDON
ANN M PRATLEY

FREEDOM
OF
FLIGHT
TRINITY
ANN M PRATLEY

FREEDOM
OF
FLIGHT
ANN M PRATLEY

CHRISTIAN
(FREEDOM OF FLIGHT SERIES - BOOK #1)

Twenty four year old Christian Shaw has a good life. He's had a rocky ride with being charged for a crime he didn't commit, but he's come out on the other side, older and wiser. He has good friends who've stood by him. He has family who love him. However there's something about Christian that he's never understood. There's something about him that sets him apart. It has made him not want to get close to anyone.

Now someone's appeared unexpectedly. To his surprise, she's just like him. Even more importantly, she has the knowledge to help him understand more about the strange existence he lives. But is she as nice as she appears, or could she have a darker reason for seeking him out and devoting time to him?

Providing an insight into one man's strange journey of coming to grips with who he really is, 'Christian' tells a story of courage, friendship and crime solving intrigue.

BRANDON
(FREEDOM OF FLIGHT SERIES - BOOK #2)

For fifteen years, Brandon McStevens has held himself
away from everyone he knew prior to the day he turned
fourteen. That day changed his life forever. Something
happened to him that he can't explain to anyone. He feels
ashamed and embarrassed. The only way he's ever been
able to move past that and live, has been to find
somewhere else to reside.

Since leaving his family home, he has continued to live
in a small cave. Nestled high above a small coastal
community, he has come to spend most of his time
enjoying the ocean … oh, and up in the sky. He doesn't
know how it happened. He doesn't know *why* it
happened. All he knows is that despite understanding
how much hurt he must have caused when he left home
all those years ago, he now lives the only existence he
can imagine.

He's never met anyone like him. He's never *seen* anyone
like him. Until that day when that woman and her dog
saw him change, no-one had ever seen or heard of him
doing that. To this day he regrets having shown himself
like he did. But time passed and it has all been forgotten
… or has it?

Certain he's the only one like himself, he's surprised
when two people come looking for him, and have much
to tell him. Finally the time will come when he no longer
has to feel like a freak of nature … or so alone.

TRINITY
(FREEDOM OF FLIGHT SERIES - BOOK #3)

A strange series of events have been happening in cities around the southwest of the country. When one bank is robbed on a small scale, it makes the banking professionals and law enforcement curious. When a second, then a third, then a fourth are also robbed without anyone knowing how it's been done, agencies combine resources to begin the search to find out who has been doing it and how.

Trinity Love is a twenty-five-year-old woman who's been surviving week to week, doing what she can to find money for her next meal and a roof over her head. In a unique way, she needs neither. She has a level of survival instinct built into her that should enable her to live a good life on the straight and narrow. That kind of life is one that she's never wanted or sought.

Seeing the latest news broadcast about the bank thefts, Brandon McStevens notices something about it that catches his attention. Talking to his new friends, Kelly and Christian, they decide it might be worth investigating.

Embarking on their new journey of exploration to find others like them, Christian and Kelly are faced with a new type of person they've never met before. Trinity is challenging in so many ways, but is she open to meeting people like her?

FORBIDDEN CONFLICTS
SERIES

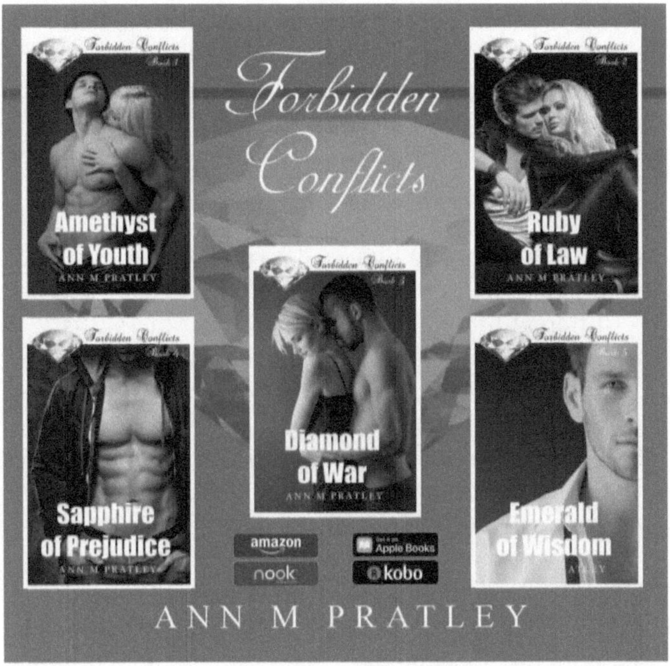

AMETHYST OF YOUTH
(FORBIDDEN CONFLICTS SERIES - BOOK #1)

The youngest member of the Stonewarden family, Charlotte (Charlie), is 18 years old. As with everyone in her family when they reach that age, she's been told that when she turns 19, she'll be recruited into the family business. She has her warning that she has one year to do anything else she wishes to do - travel, study, work. Whatever she wants to do, she has 365 days to do it. On her next birthday, her life will effectively stop being her own.

But Charlie wants nothing to do with the business. The youngest of six, with five older brothers, she wants a different life. Maybe if the family business was something normal like a retail shop or a business centered around trade, she'd feel differently. There are people who say that her family's long term history of robbing from the rich and providing to the poor is a good thing. To her, all she can see is that they are thieves. Plain and simple.

Her view is further secured when she and her older brother, Max, are shot at in a local supermarket. Seeing Max lying in blood and later lying unmoving in hospital in a coma, pushes her further in her resolve to find a way to not take part in the activities of her father and brothers.

At the shootout she is saved by a checkout operator, Ash. Whilst building their friendship Charlie will learn things about her family that she didn't particularly wish to know. She will hear more and more that she can't share with Ash, and the more she learns, the wider the gap will become.

In years she's young, but having lost her mother when she was a child, Charlie has an older soul. The possibilities she'll be presented with during her final year of her own, will push her in her considerations of how she really wants her life to be. She wants one thing. Her strict ex-military father wants another. The dynamics of her new friendship will pull her in a third direction.

How will she chose what's right for her? And what would she have to do to break free from the chains that she can see her father wants to place around her for the rest of her life?

REVIEWERS SAY:
"This was a good clean romance with plenty of action to further the story along ... will make you ponder about life's situations, their actions and reactions, and how the decisions of past generations can affect the current ones. You'll be glad you read it!"

"... loved this book! It took me by surprise-great from start to finish! I don't normally read crime family dramas, but I love NA/coming-of-age novels. Charlie is on the cusp of being inducted into her family's Robin Hood-esque biz, but she doesn't want that. She isn't sure what, exactly, she does want...just not THAT. Her connection with Ash furthers that disconnect, and they stumble through the beginnings of young love together ... secrets and family craziness threaten their romance at every turn ...an awesome start to the Forbidden Conflicts series!"

"A wonderful read. A timeless push and pull between our own wants and our family's wants. Will she follow the path her family wants or will she follow her own path?"

RUBY OF LAW
(FORBIDDEN CONFLICTS SERIES - BOOK #2)

For generations the Leadbetters have lived off crime. For as long as any of them know, fathers and mothers have taught sons and daughters how to succeed in the criminal world, primarily through theft.

Phillip Leadbetter is 29 and has devoted his whole life so far to doing what his father and mother have told him to do. The sacrifice for doing that is that he still lives at home and he hasn't yet met anyone who he believes could accept the man that he is, because of his family.

One night a potential tragedy brings him into the path of Daisy, an up and coming professional in the legal sector. Seeing him as her knight in shining armor, she can't stop thinking about the rugged guy who saved her. She's also very pleased when fate brings their paths to cross again.

Getting to know one another, both leave out major details about who they are. She doesn't want him to know she's a lawyer because some people just don't like lawyers. He doesn't want to tell her about his family and their long history of criminal activity.

How then will things turn when they meet up in a courthouse, each learning in that moment who the other really is? How will they deal with the fact that she is on one side of the law, and he is very definitely on the other?

DIAMOND OF WAR
(FORBIDDEN CONFLICTS SERIES - BOOK #3)

James Stonewarden is a playboy. He has been since the moment he first started to notice girls. He loves them all, and they all love him. Why would he want to get himself into a relationship?

Sasha Leadbetter's a hot-headed young woman, known to the law for her quick temper and harsh ways. She isn't one to mess with - especially with the way she keeps a blade in her pocket. To her it's her security. It's something that makes her feel safe and comfortable. She's had it for so long that it's nothing for her to pull it out and hold it to someone's throat without any conscious thought.

Unaware of who each other are, or how their families are distantly interconnected through crime, the chance of James Stonewarden meeting Sasha Leadbetter is slim. But it happens.

A playboy and a young woman who has the mentality to kill. What kind of recipe could that result in? And what will happen when James identifies a car at Sasha's family home, that matches the description his sister Charlie gave after the supermarket shooting months earlier?

SAPPHIRE OF PREJUDICE
(FORBIDDEN CONFLICTS SERIES - BOOK #4)

Greg and Rhett. They've grown up together since they were teenagers. They've fought together. They've stolen together. They've even loved women together. But something deeper has existed in one of them for years. He's hidden it well. Being part of the great Leadbetter gang and family, the prejudice of certain situations has always been loudly expressed by many of its members - too many, and certainly enough to make anyone fearful of what would happen if feelings were revealed and brought out into the open.

A night has passed when finally, in a moment of wondering if he'd survive till morning, Rhett's taken the chance and kissed the person of his desire.
Given their circumstances, what can they do,
and where can they go?

Meanwhile, as Phillip Leadbetter continues on his path of happiness with his Daisy, someone from her past has grown obsessed with her and wants her back. To what degree will he put into effect a plan to get her back, and get Phillip out of her life forever?

~~ NOTE: This book does contain adult sexual content and LOTS of swear words.

EMERALD OF WISDOM
(FORBIDDEN CONFLICTS SERIES - BOOK #5)

When Mitchell Stonewarden lost his wife to cancer more than a decade ago, he vowed to never give his heart to anyone else. With all of his children now adults, and a new generation of Stonewardens having already begun, he's finally started to wonder - does he really want to be alone for the rest of his life? The handover of the family business to his oldest son, Vic, has seemed to be free of difficulty or issues - but has it? Mitchell knows little of his oldest son's private life away from the family. He is surprised by what is brought to his attention that he had no idea about.

While Mitchell finally starts to move on into a new chapter of his life, another of his sons - Max - is on his own path of discovery in life and in love. Previously well-known as 'Romeo' to his family and peers, he begins to wonder if Christy - a surprising addition to his life - has grown to become more important to him than any other young woman he's ever met. When her work at a homeless shelter tests the boundaries of her safety, Max's commitment to her is also tested, making him wonder if he will, indeed, end up hurting her.

Meanwhile, on the other side of town, the Leadbetter family is shattered by an unexpected turn of events that leaves Stacey wondering if she is going to lose the man she's loved for more than three decades...

KNIGHT OF DESIRE

Cecily, Azura and Maynard have grown up together from childhood. In many ways they've always felt equal ... except for Maynard being a prince, that is.

After her two closest friends find each other in love and then marriage, taking on the ruling of a kingdom, Cecily finds herself questioning if love is in her future. Over time, it becomes apparent that she certainly has caught someone's eye. He is a knight and he is known to be a rogue, but can the handsome Sir Henry capture the fair heart of Cecily, and push her fears aside?

Knight of Desire is a simple old-fashioned light-hearted short-read romance. There is no adult content or violence in this story. This story is also not an essential book in the Four Swords series, being set years prior to Blade of Envy beginning.

BLADE OF ENVY
(FOUR SWORDS SERIES - BOOK #1)

They expected quite a different kind of destruction...

In the realm of the House of Mordasini, the three royal offspring of King Maynard and Queen Azura are beginning their journeys into adulthood.

As the eldest, Prince Aldin, starts to obsess about his future role as the next king, so also begins an obsession about his younger brother. Torn between wanting to be the one who rules over everyone else, but also wanting the life that is being set up for his brother, Aldin begins a journey of envy that grows darker as time passes.

Meanwhile, as one brother ruminates about the life of the other, their younger sister, Princess Semera, appears to grow ill. In the quiet of her deep slumber, something surprising begins to happen as, from a distance, she unknowingly becomes someone else's focus.

BLADE OF LOVE
(FOUR SWORDS SERIES - BOOK #2)

In the kingdom of the House of Mordasini, a future king
is waiting for the day to come when his father will die.
While there's nothing to suggest that King Maynard will
be leaving this world anytime soon, his oldest son,
Aldin, increasingly desires to be the one on the throne.
With the darkness that has been residing in his soul since
he was a child, ideas begin to flow inside of Aldin's
mind. All around him, there are things happening that go
against his idea of how the realm should be run. In
particular, the realization that his father has granted
permission to his brother, Prince Iztal, to wed, is
something that adds to Aldin's hatred for his brother - a
hatred that has grown into an intense obsession.

While brothers continue to share their volatile
relationship, their sister continues to experience signs
that a beast will soon arrive in the realm, eager to cause
destruction. Everyone thinks they are ready for the
beast's return, but are they? To stop such destruction
from happening, two princes who have no time for one
another must unite, but can they?

PAINFUL DELIVERANCE
(PAINFUL DELIVERANCE SERIES - BOOK #1)

She just wasn't made for inflicting pain.

She knows it is nothing abnormal. She knows others enjoy it. But with every new level of pain he directs her to deliver to him, Alexis feels another piece of her soul die. He has wealth and he has power, and she knows he won't easily let her go.

But she has to leave. Escape. Move on. Forget. She has reached her limit of what she can do. The plans are in place to get away. She just has to hope that wherever she goes - whoever she meets - she won't find herself in exactly the same situation again.

DARKNESS OF HEART
(PAINFUL DELIVERANCE SERIES - BOOK #2)

She thought he'd stopped looking. He hadn't.

She got away from him to start a new life. She moved on. But in his mind, he still loves her and needs her. He still believes that she loves him. That she is meant to be his. That he is meant to be hers.

He will not give up searching for her. He will not give up *fighting* for her. He will pursue her and stop at nothing to get her back. But it will come at a cost … a sacrifice much greater than he will see coming. A sacrifice that will finally wake him up and bring him back to stark reality.

REVIEWERS SAY:
"… author did a great job of making brief references from the first book. Lincoln, Lexi and Alexis are back, though perhaps the most complex character is Diana … definitely written for a mature audience … the author is a great storyteller and writes with an easy to read style … very easy for me to recommend this book with 5stars."

"This story continued the journey of Alexis, Anthony and Lincoln while giving us a new perspective into the repercussions of Lincoln and Alexis's relationship: from the POV of Lincoln's wife Diana! I loved her addition to the story's … kept the tension of the story just right, balancing the calm new life Alexis has been building and keeping the reader engaged."

"It is a book of courage, the courage to leave everything you know behind, the courage to change, the courage to face your fears, and the courage to face the unknown."

FRIENDSHIP OF DESIRE
(PAINFUL DELIVERANCE SERIES - BOOK #3)

Tom and Samantha. Feisty friends from childhood who feel like they know each other inside out, until the day comes when one of them suggests they go to a BDSM club together, and become formal play partners. Pushing the limits of what each of them can individually stand in their lifelong friendship, they attract and repel like magnets, until the time comes when they must choose how they will relate to one another - and what kind of relationship they will go on to have in the future.

Whilst on this journey of discovery, the two of them meet and make a new friend - Alexis. A young woman with a hidden and secretive past, and a mystery surrounding the relationship she has - or has had - with a renowned business entrepreneur who begins to integrate himself into Samantha's life, unknown to any of them whether he has done it for him, or for her … or for Alexis, being the mysterious link from his past.

REVIEWERS SAY:
"While this book is billed as the third in a series, I would classify it more as a spin-off … I enjoyed this book. Samantha and Tom's relationship was sweet. Their exploration and experimentation, and how it stressed the boundaries of their (frustratingly) platonic friendship was fun to read about. Fans of Ms. Pratley's first books in the Painful Deliverance series will surely enjoy this more intimate peek into Samantha and Tom's relationship."

THE GOLDEN DESIRES
(THE GOLDEN DESIRES SERIES - BOOK #1)

He wanted to escape. They needed to survive.

When Isabella starts to dream of a stranger, she's awakened inside with feelings she has never felt before. She knows he's not someone she's ever seen before, and he is not of her village. He is a stranger, and she's desperate to determine if he is real or he is a part of her imagination.

Far away a businessman desperate to escape the noise and stress of the city, embarks on a journey to find peace and the solitude he increasingly needs and desires. But at his destination he will find much, much more.

REVIEWERS SAY:
"I found myself drawn to keep reading ... almost as if reading a compelling action/adventure because the pacing was so excellent. And... ahem... the love scenes are quite well written, too ... I look forward to reading the sequel..."

"The author paints such a vivid picture of life in this idyllic community that one begins to think it may actually exist ... extremely well-written ... perfect for anyone who is looking for a romance with a hint of paranormal mystery."

"The concept behind this story was intriguing and very sexy ... Fireworks and all out romance, followed by some interesting obstacles, but they are overcome, because well...it's love. What I loved about this read was the fairytale like narration with a sci-fi/fantasy kick; it made me feel like I was part of the story..."

"... magical quality was a nice twist, delving into the realm of fantasy romance ... the author's style was well suited to the tone of the world she has created. Did it leave me hungry for the next installment? Absolutely!"

THE GOLDEN SUPREMACY
(THE GOLDEN DESIRES SERIES - BOOK #2)

What is lying in wait, eager to destroy them?

Over distance and time they met and fell in love, choosing to live together in an ancient village of peace and harmony. Then the battle had happened - a fight between good and evil; the warmth of fire and the cold of ice. They thought they had won. But had they?

Trent and Isabella start to feel that the entity that had tried to destroy them might not have been defeated after all. But rather, perhaps it is lying in wait for another opportunity to strike.

What is it?
And who is its puppet now?

THE GOLDEN UNITY
(GOLDEN DESIRES SERIES - BOOK #3)

Cesare is the golden child of the village. His vibrant yellow hair is unlike the color of anyone else's. He is a cheerful child who in the eyes of some can do no wrong.

Esmeralda is the product of two biological parents who have something buried deep within them. Something that makes them easy to manipulate by the being that has not given up on wanting to destroy the ancient village. The young lass with the blue-black hair is looked upon as an alternative child. She captures attention and intrigues the villagers. When they look at her, sometimes they feel like they're looking at a puzzle that confuses them and they cannot solve. It's impossible to determine why but there's just something *different* about Esmeralda.

Despite them being opposites in nature and appearance, the two have grown up together as best friends, just as their parents did before them. The goodness of Cesare showers a level of kindness and friendship on Esmeralda that she has never been able to turn away from. The difference of Esmeralda has always held Cesare's attention. Between them they have found a balance that holds them together as friends. But what will happen as they move into their time as young adults? They are unknowing as yet that they are meant to be paired, whilst at the same time they are meant to be adversaries.

What does the puppet master have planned now? And how will these two gifted youth react to someone trying to manipulate them against their will?

A third strike from the puppet master. Will it win in its plan of attack this time?

TOTAL FREEDOM
(TOTAL FREEDOM SERIES - BOOK #1)

For Debbie King, life began feeling like it was all too difficult. She would never achieve, she would never have friends, and she would simply never fit in. But when she meets someone new who seems just like her, with low self-esteem and no belief in themselves and what they have to offer, Debbie finds the strength to focus more on them and less on herself.

So begins an incredible journey of friendship and love that will be tested by other people entering their world, and the shared passion they have for their musical talents and career together. It is a deep friendship that will be tested over and over again by events and an ongoing uncertainty over what their relationship really should really be like.

REVIEWERS SAY:
"The overall story was great and hooked me right in. I had to stay with them for the entire journey ... you know it's a good story when you wish it didn't have to end."

"... an incredible job developing complex characters that are emotionally scarred and then allowing the reader to really understand their pain ... a terrific coming of age story surrounding a triangle of young characters, Debbie, Craig and Steven."

"Covered a lot of different things that can happen as we grow and was appealing for that reason."

TOTAL NEW BEGINNINGS
(TOTAL FREEDOM SERIES - BOOK #2)

In her early adulthood Debbie made a choice. She had two men who loved her. She chose one. She lost the friendship of the other.

Twenty years on, horrific tragedy strikes. Mother to three grown children, she has to find the strength to be there for them while pushing her own grief aside. Dealing with the loss of the man who has been by her side for two decades pushes her into depression. Every day seems harder to deal with than the last. The feeling of loss is further heightened by finding her husband's lifetime of journals. Hesitant at first to look inside them, she eventually does. Almost instantly she regrets that decision. In the years of her husband's writing she reads things that lead her to seriously question whether she ever really knew him at all, or if they had actually been strangers for two decades.

The combination of the loss of her husband, and the uncertainty about who he really was, pushes her to retire into a dark room and have no desire to leave. She wants to shut out the world. She wants to not believe what she knows in her heart is reality.

With her youngest daughter, Poppy, still living at home, Debbie is eventually pulled from the darkness by her daughter's pleas. Finally the dark days start to fade and Debbie can start to see the sun shining once more. Finally she can find the strength to keep going. Finally she can start to move into a period of recovery and growth. Finally she can accept that it's okay to accept help and lean on others.

As she starts rediscovering her ability to embrace life again, results appear from her daughter's determination to help her mother. Someone from her past is brought back into her life. A friendship is re-established. It's time to let go of the past and begin a new future. It's time for total new beginnings.

Did you ever hear the words in your head … 'what if'? What if you chose one path earlier in life but later had the chance to walk down the path previously unchosen? Would you?

ANN M PRATLEY
Finding Himself Again

FINDING HIMSELF AGAIN

In a small seaside area of Sydney, Australia, 28-year-old Tom Santini has recently returned to the outside world after ten long years in jail following an error of judgment in his youth. Readjustment hasn't been easy but luck has taken a turn for him. The woman that his brother, Graham, has been seeing is a woman with connections. Through her, Tom has finally found an employer who will give an ex-criminal a chance to start over. It hasn't been an easy six months since his release, but Tom is learning to face his situation with reality and step up to take responsibility for his decisions.

Settled in his job at Toby's Stop'n'Dine, Tom's attention is captured by a young woman who enters. She's beautiful and alluring but, seeing and talking to her, he can deeply sense her being on the run from something … or someone.

Cat is smart, sexy and a woman who will make him wonder if he does, in fact, have a chance at being happy in love, despite his past. But why does she spook so easily? What - or who - is she on the run from? Tom knows that whatever happens, he has to think before he acts. He is determined to do things differently when it comes to dealing with difficult situations. He's already missed out on so much. He cannot go back to prison.

What can he do to calm and keep safe the woman who he so recently met but already has made a difference in his life? How can he save the woman with a deep-seated passion that drives him crazy…

THANK YOU!

Writing is something that I love to do, whether in romance, crime solving, paranormal, time travel, or something far more spicier, and I do appreciate the time you've invested into reading this story.

Every second month, I send out a newsletter to my subscribed readers, enabling them to learn about new releases and freebies, and take part in the odd opportunity to win items such as books, Amazon gift cards, and Kindle e-readers. If this sounds like something you might be interested in, please sign up at http://eepurl.com/ca559H

~~~~~

If you would like to make contact with me, please:
Follow me on Bookbub
https://www.bookbub.com/authors/ann-m-pratley

Follow Me On Twitter
https://twitter.com/runkiwiwriter

Thank you,
Ann M Pratley
~~~~~